THOUSAND OAKS LIBRARY

S0-AAA-165

3 2052 00821 6734

JAN 2003

8/05   8(1) 4/05

DISCARD

Collection Management

4/06	10-1	1/06
3/20 11	19—1	9/08
6/9/10		

THOUSAND OAKS LIBRARY
1401 E. Janss Road
Thousand Oaks, CA 91362

I♥69

OTHER NOVELS BY ANN RINALDI

Cast Two Shadows
The American Revolution in the South

An Acquaintance with Darkness

Hang a Thousand Trees with Ribbons
The Story of Phillis Wheatley

Keep Smiling Through

The Secret of Sarah Revere

Finishing Becca
A Story about Peggy Shippen and Benedict Arnold

The Fifth of March
A Story of the Boston Massacre

A Break with Charity
A Story about the Salem Witch Trials

A Ride into Morning
The Story of Tempe Wick

I♥69

ANN RINALDI

The Coffin

GULLIVER BOOKS

HARCOURT, INC.

San Diego   New York   London

THE FEUD BETWEEN

THE HATFIELDS

AND THE McCOYS

Copyright © 1999 by Ann Rinaldi

All rights reserved. No part of this publication may be reproduced or
transmitted in any form or by any means, electronic or mechanical, including
photocopy, recording, or any information storage and retrieval system,
without permission in writing from the publisher.

Requests for permission to make copies of any part of the work should be mailed
to the following address: Permissions Department, Harcourt, Inc.,
6277 Sea Harbor Drive, Orlando, Florida 32887-6777.

www.harcourt.com

First Gulliver Books paperback edition 2001
Gulliver Books is a trademark of Harcourt, Inc.,
registered in the United States of America and/or other jurisdictions.

The Library of Congress has cataloged the hardcover edition as follows:
Rinaldi, Ann.
The coffin quilt: the feud between the Hatfields and the McCoys/
Ann Rinaldi.
p.   cm.—(Great Episodes)
"Gulliver Books."
Summary: In the 1880s, young Fanny McCoy witnesses the growth of a
terrible and violent feud between her Kentucky family and the West Virginia
Hatfields, complicated by her older sister Roseanna's romance with a Hatfield.
1. Hatfield-McCoy feud—Juvenile fiction. [1. Hatfield-McCoy feud—
Fiction.   2. Vendetta—Fiction.   3. Mountain life—Appalachian Region—
Fiction.   4. Appalachian Region—Fiction.]   I. Title.
PZ7.R459Co   1999
[Fic]—dc21   99-14455
ISBN 0-15-202015-2
ISBN 0-15-216450-2 pb

Text set in Stempel Garamond
Designed by Trina Stahl

C E G H F D B

YA FIC

For my daughter-in-law Susan,
my biggest fan

The Coffin Quilt

Prologue

DECEMBER 3, 1889

TODAY THEY HANGED Ellison Mounts. He was a half-wit and his people are dirt-poor and simple, but he didn't deserve to die. I know it and some others do, too. But when they put Ma on the witness stand at his trial, they shut her up. Said she still wasn't right in the head after what happened to her. The prosecuting attorney even called Ma a liar, and I thought Pa would shoot him on the spot. And they sentenced the half-wit Mounts to death then and there for what happened the night the Hatfields' gang attacked our house and did the killings.

All of Eastern Kentucky came out for his hanging. There hasn't been such a holiday in Pikeville since I can't remember when. Women wore their best homespun. The streets were so crowded you could scarce walk. Brandy was ordered in from Catlettsburg. The moonshine was supplied by my brother Floyd, who's more than a fair hand at the making of it, who uses copper for his stills and not tin, and who wasn't above selling a few of his hand-whittled toys to the young people on the side.

By ten o'clock most of the men were pretty well in their cups. And there were McCoys all over the place, armed to their eyebrows, wearing leather belts crossed on their chests, loaded with shot, and with pistols strapped on their legs under their trousers, and rifles, long and mean. People were saying that old Devil Anse and the Hatfields were coming any minute to stop the hanging.

People waited for it like the Second Coming. And there was Pa, worn down and looking older than I ever recollect, giving his men orders, sending some to Chloe Creek and others to Coon Creek, to head the Hatfields off if they came.

I met my used-to-be teacher, Ambrose Cuzlin. He bought me a cup of coffee from a street seller. "Too bad about Mounts," he said to me. He'd had Ellison in school. "How's your ma doing, Fanny?"

"She's middling well," I said.

He bought me some gingerbread, too, from an old lady selling it "one fer a nickel and three fer a dime."

"You thought any more about taking the exam for normal school?" he asked me.

I looked around me at the growing excitement of the crowd. *Normal school*, I thought. *I might go just for the sound of it.* "I'm still studying on it," I said.

"I'll bring over some more books. The exam is at the end of the month. There isn't much more time, Fanny."

"I'll let you know before Christmas," I promised.

"Oh no! A band! They're not going to play music, are they?"

"Sure they are. It wouldn't be a hanging without one, would it?"

The musicians were playing "Blackeyed Susie" and the guards, all McCoys, were leading Mounts to the scaffold. Everybody got quiet. The sheriff asked Mounts if he had any last words.

"I never kilt her," he said.

I think the sheriff knew it, too. Same as we all know that birds listen and chipmunks gossip, that there's witchcraft in the hills around here, that you don't ever go into a person's yard without first giving a holler, and that Hatfields and McCoys will always hate each other.

I turned away at the hanging. I heard something crack. A woman next to us, about six months into her delicate condition, fainted. Mr. Cuzlin picked her up, took a flask out of his pocket, and poured some whiskey down her throat.

"Oh God," she said, "I'll never forget the sound of that man's neck breaking."

"You had no business coming here, the way you are." Mr. Cuzlin scolded her like he'd do to us in the schoolroom. I expected him to tell her to go sit in a corner.

"Likely your baby will be marked now," a woman standing nearby said.

"Nonsense," Mr. Cuzlin said. "The mountain people and their superstitions." Like he wasn't mountain people, too, come from Virginia to survey the land and stayed on to teach. "Did you ever hear such nonsense, Fanny McCoy?"

"I've heard such and more. And you know it."

We were friends. Sometimes I thought he was the only real friend I had anymore, though I saw him only on occasion. After the hanging he asked me was I all right, and was there anything he could do for me. I wished there were. I wished he could open *Pike's Arithmetic* and tell me the universe is all made up of numbers, and everything adds up and makes sense. I said no, thanked him, and started home, disgusted with myself for coming. It was too cold, the world too shivering naked and howling fierce. And made colder by the eager looks on the faces of those who had come to see a man hanged, rather than stay home by their fires and make venison stew or nail together a wooden toy for children who would soon be out in a world that hanged a person who wasn't guilty.

And I was worried about Ma, left on her lone as she was in the house.

———

FIRST THING I did was seek her out in the small mean parlor. The fire in the grate was down, so I built it up. Then I made her some sassafras tea. She was sitting there all alone working on her Friendship quilt. That would be funny if it weren't so sad, Ma working on a Friendship quilt when nobody in my family even knows anymore what friendship is about. If they ever did.

It made me think of the quilt I had hidden upstairs under my bed, and the promise I'd made when it was first given to me. And the promise I made to myself about it. And how I had to break the first promise and keep the second. Soon. Very soon now.

Ma looked so frail sitting there. It was the pitifullest thing. She never has been right since she had her hip and arm and skull smashed that night two years ago now. It gives me the jimjams every time I see her.

"Is Mounts dead?" she asked.

"Yes."

"I'll pray for his soul."

I was sure she would. Only thing I didn't know was what side of her tree stump would the pebble named Mounts end up on? The saved side? Or the damned?

First thing she did when we moved to this house on East Main Street was find a flat stone out back where she put the pebbles of everybody she prayed for. She hobbles out there every so often to change the pebbles to different sides. I don't want to know anymore what side I'm on. Me and Ma have fussed too much at each other in this house. I hate it here. I miss our place on Blackberry Fork. But it's all gone, burned to the ground.

I have places to go. I don't have to stay here. I can go stay with my brother Jim and his family. Or my brother Sam. I can go to normal school like Mr. Cuzlin wants. Onliest reason I haven't bestirred myself yet is for Ma. Pa's away all day running the Big Sandy ferry from Pikeville to Ferguson's Creek. My sister Adelaide has become a granny woman, and she's only two years older than I am, eighteen. She tends people when they get down sick and delivers babies.

Forget Trinvilla. She's just become too downright uppity.

"Did Devil Anse come, like your pa feared?" Ma asked.

"No. He never showed, Ma."

She sighed. "Adelaide sent a note she might be in for supper."

"There's enough food. I'll go fix things." I went to the kitchen to start supper. As usual I had to struggle with the cast-iron stove. I hate it. I miss our old wood range at home, with its warming closets on top where you could put biscuits at breakfast and they'd stay warm all day. I miss the fresh trout brother Calvin would bring in, the honey from brother Pharmer's bees, the raccoons brother Bud and his dogs would bring home from a day's hunting.

We belonged to a place on Blackberry Fork. And it was a staying thing. Now it's gone. Oh, I can do some ciphering and know, bit by bit, how it was taken away. But that doesn't put any sense on it. And today I'm toting such a misery about it that I've come right to my room to write in the blank book Mr. Cuzlin once gave me.

I write to improve my penmanship for normal school. I have to give Mr. Cuzlin an answer soon. That man's been good to me. But I can't bestir myself to go unless I rid myself of the poison inside me. My writing is kind of like Adelaide's blood purifier that she's always giving Ma. And besides, I don't aim to be like our sheep, so shy that if a wild animal attacks, they just lie down and get ready to die. There's been too much dying around these parts for my liking. I'm plumb sick of it. And I don't even know if it's all over yet. So I'm going to write what happened. The way it was for me, at least. The way it was all my life. Since I was a knee baby of seven.

Chapter One

1880

I ASKED MY brother Tolbert about our sheep once, why they do like they do, being on the one hand so brave the way they spend weeks a-wanderin' in the mountains, and on the other hand so meek.

It was the time me and Tolbert were sent by Pa to fetch my sister Roseanna home, after she first run off. I was staying with Tolbert and Mary for a spell because my sister Alifair had tried to kill me again. For the third time. This time she held my head under the pump in the yard until I near drowned, because I'd left school without permission. Once before she spilled hot bacon fat on me, which she said was an accident. I had to wear a cut potato bound on my arm for a week. Another time she switched my legs until I couldn't walk. Both times for sassing her. Alifair is the oldest girl, and as such demands respect. And Ma and Pa turn a deaf ear when I say she's trying to kill me. But they know it to be true. Else why would they send me to live with Tolbert for a spell to get me away from her?

The why of it nobody has figured. Ma says Alifair has the light of holiness. Isn't she working at church with the healing group? She hasn't healed anybody yet, but she's darned near killed me. I think she has powers, all right. Evil. But the good part is I get to stay with Tolbert and Mary when Alifair's light of holiness gets too bright. Tolbert is my favorite brother, not only because he cusses a lot in public and gets fined a dollar a cuss for it, but because he likes to dance and sing, and fight, too. His pebble in Mama's prayer garden is always on the side of the damned. It never bothers Tolbert any.

In his house you can read *Oliver Twist* of a Sunday without Mama saying you'd burn in hellfire forever for violating the Sabbath. And Mary treats me like I was near grown. I know they want me to live with them regular-like. Tolbert asked Pa once if I could. They'd send me to school, teach me to observe God's laws, take me to Sunday Meeting, everything. Pa said no. He doesn't like to let go of what's his.

Anyways, we were riding over to West Virginia to fetch Ro home. Pa sent Tolbert because he's so level in the head, and Tolbert took me because I was close to Roseanna. In this family, being so many of us, the young 'uns sort of attach themselves to an older one. Trinvilla and Adelaide belong to Alifair. Bill follows Bud around like a coon pup.

"Why do our sheep just lie down and get ready to die when they're attacked?" I asked Tolbert. "Why don't they fight?"

"Got nuthin' to fight with," he said. "And they know it."

"It's not fair that God didn't give them anything to fight with," I said. "Most other creatures can defend themselves."

"Maybe God was tryin' to show us that there's two kinds of creatures in this world. Those that fight and those that don't," he said.

"You mean the sheep are like Mama? They'd rather pray?"

"Maybe," he said. "But that don't make 'em stupid. You think Ma's stupid?"

One thing Tolbert wouldn't hold with was my sassing Ma or Pa. Even though he knew they were both wrong about things sometimes. So I said no. Because I didn't ever want to earn myself the rough side of Tolbert's tongue.

"The sheep aren't stupid," he said. "Look how they know to come home after bein' out in the mountains for weeks."

Our sheep come home at least once a month. You open your eyes one morning and there they all just are, come for salt. Pa or one of the boys would give them some, and then they'd be gone again. All on their own.

I was kind of hoping that's the way it would be with Roseanna, that I'd just open my eyes one morning and she'd be there in the bed next to me. I missed her something powerful. "Do they come home only for the salt?"

" 'Pears to be so."

"For nothing else?"

He looked at me. Tolbert was the tallest and he was

fair of hair and eyes, but it was what was in those eyes that held you. He didn't say much. But when he did, you listened. "What's goin' on in that head of yours, Fanny?"

"Well, I just thought maybe they come home because they know they belong here," I said. "And they want to make sure it'll all still be here for them. The house and us, I mean."

"They come home for the salt," he said. "But I like to think that all creatures want to come home sooner or later."

"Do you think Ro will come home, then?" I asked.

He didn't say anything for a minute. Just kept his eyes on the trail ahead, like he does sometimes. "Hope she's got the sense of our sheep," he said.

"Tolbert, why does Alifair hate me so?"

"She doesn't hate you, Fanny. She hates herself. Hates that she's lived twenty-two years and don't know what she's about. Hates that you're just a young 'un and still have the chance to find out. My guess is once she forgets about this healing business and pays mind to that young Will Bectal who wants to court her, she'll be a happier woman."

"Does she have the light of holiness? When she comes at me I want to kick her or bite her. But how can I if she's got it?"

"She's got the light of too much Ma. She should have got out from under Ma's shadow and been married years ago. Ma's a good woman, but she's trying to make Alifair into herself all over. She's got no light and no holiness, and the sooner she finds it out, the better we'll all be. So you kick and bite her all you want to defend yourself.

Onliest reason I tell you this is because Alifair's been so hard on you. Not so you don't reverence Ma. You understand?"

I said yes. And since he was explaining things so good I thought I'd push further. "Why do Hatfields and McCoys hate each other?"

He grunted. "I hold it goes back to when Pa lost his sow and his pigs, two years ago. Ma says no, before that even. During The War Amongst Us, Pa's younger brother Harmon was murdered by bushwhackers. Everybody says it was old Devil Anse Hatfield and his Wildcats. You see, in 1863, Virginia's western counties broke away and became West Virginia. When men from that area got to come home on leave, they just didn't go back. They'd been fighting for their own ground, and now it was Union blue ground. So they formed their own Home Guard in West Virginia and stayed Confederate. Called themselves the Wildcats.

"And those were the people, headed up by Devil Anse, who shot and killed Pa's brother Harmon when he came home for a Christmas furlough. Shot him for coming out for the Union."

"So it started with the war?"

"Let's say the war just continued, only in a different way," Tolbert said.

"Ma always said it was the fortunes of war that made the men hereabouts so lawless and disorderly."

"Lawless and disorderly be danged. There's nothing lawless about wanting your own sow and pigs back," Tolbert muttered. Only he didn't say *danged*. "It's just in the McCoy blood to make right a wrong done to you or yourn. And to uphold the family honor while you're doing it. People around here, for the most part, are very serious about honor, though nobody more than the McCoys. It goes back to our ancestors in Scotland, who were Highland Celts. That Celtic strain runs right through our blood."

I looked down at my hands holding the reins, at the tiny blue veins I could trace on their backs. I wondered what Celtic blood looked like and how it was different from other people's blood. I liked Tolbert's explanations. They made sense. Especially about Alifair. It was good to know she didn't have the light of holiness. Next time she started on me I'd kick and bite her good. Then let her heal herself and see how good she'd do.

Chapter Two

1880

THE FIRST TIME I saw Yeller Thing was right before Ro ran off. And from then on I saw him just before every bad thing happened to any of us. I was the only one who ever did see him. And I haven't seen him since she's gone.

Yeller Thing was the most terrible creature you'd ever want to run into in these mountains. Stinking worse than a skunk. I never could lay my mind hold of what he was so I could tell my brothers, who all went gunning for him. Oh, they heard him, all right, and smelled him, thrashing around out there in the woods. But they never saw him like I did. He wasn't a painter cat, they said, and he wasn't a bear. He was something nobody could explain.

Except me. Because Yeller Thing came for me, to warn me of what was to happen to us, of how there was evil amongst us. But not only that, he came to show me how evil often had the face of beauty and good. Like Alifair with her light of holiness. And Ro with her pretty looks and ways. And sometimes evil even attached itself to good, to draw strength from it. Like it did with Mama, in spite of, and maybe even because of her prayerful ways.

But I was too young. I didn't know. I thought it was just a haint, like people sometimes see in these parts. I thought it was enough to make a cross in the dirt with my toe, spit in it, and make a good wish every time I left the house so Yeller Thing couldn't get me.

And all the time evil was there. In our house. And had got us all already.

––––––

DOES ANYBODY KNOW what it's like to have an older sister like Roseanna? So purty that just being next to her is better than a piece of rock candy? Just being around her you didn't need a spring tonic. When she walked by everybody looked. Then looked again. Once wasn't enough. Ma said that she could turn a person into a pillar of salt. Or if not that, then an addled idiot.

I wanted to be like her. The way she dressed, walked, tossed her hair was just perfect. She sang, made a pie, diapered a baby, even slopped the hogs better than anybody.

I can still smell the glycerin and rosewater she used. Sometimes of a dark night I'll smell it in the house just like she's there, roaming around in her white night-dress.

Sometimes I think she still is.

———

I SUPPOSE I ought to put down about Pa's sow and pigs, just to keep things straight.

It was 1878 and I was five, so I'm just putting down what was told to me. But here it is. Like every other family in these mountains, we raise hogs. And like the sheep, we let them go in the hills to forage. This is done right before hog-killing time. The nuts fatten them up. And so they don't get mixed up, every hog owner marks his own.

Pa's mark was a slit in the right ear and an overbit in the left. But when time came to go fetch those hogs home, Pharmer, Calvin, and Bill, three of my brothers, couldn't find them. As it turned out, one of those hogs, Pinky, was my pet, even though I knew she'd have to be slaughtered and eaten. I trudged along after my brothers and called and called for Pinky, but I was just a mite glad she wouldn't be found. I hoped she'd stay free until after hog-killing time. Then I could have her for another year, and maybe convince Pa to let me keep her.

My brother Bill was twelve at the time, already given to long periods of silence, and he played the fiddle sweet as Gabriel's horn. He was on his way home from Stringtown, where he'd been playing for a family wedding, when he passed Floyd Hatfield's cabin and saw Pa's pigs, one of them Pinky. Soon's he came home, Pa was off with his gun, like The War Amongst Us was still going on.

Of course Floyd wouldn't give back those pigs. So Pa had the Justice of the Peace make a warrant, and Floyd was charged with stealing those pigs. You'd think that would be nobody's business but Floyd's and my pa's, wouldn't you? Not in these parts. Seems every McCoy in Pike County and beyond was already loading his gun because their kin's hogs had been stolen.

Stealing a hog is a serious business. There isn't any part of the hog my family doesn't use—head for stew or scrapple, tongue to be boiled in water and sliced and served cold, the liver for pudding, the backbone, tail, and ribs can be barbecued or made into stews, and of course the lard for fat.

Some people eat the lights, or the lungs. We feed them to the dogs.

So you can see that a hog thief is the low-down-est, bloodsucking-est snake there is.

Mama, of course, right off told Pa he shouldn't of brought charges. "Trouble will come of it," she said. Mama sees trouble behind every red maple tree. She can't help it. What I can't figure is how anybody can be walking with the Lord for so many years now and be afeared all the time. She's always singing that song, "If Everybody Was Like Jesus What a Wonderful World This Would Be." She's had her feet washed in Meeting, just like the women in the Bible washed the feet of Jesus. It's an honor that doesn't come to everybody.

Anyways, the judge was a Hatfield but the jury was both Hatfields and McCoys. The judge said he'd be fair if everybody put away their pistols. The jury was split right down the middle on whose hogs they were, so they took a vote. The last one to decide was Selkirk McCoy, who was married to a Hatfield. Selkirk said the hogs belonged to Floyd, and that was it.

A fight almost broke out in court, but Pa abided by the judge's decision. And I had to give up Pinky.

Then Squirrel Huntin' Sam McCoy comes into it.

It's as much of our history as the fact that Pa and Ma are first cousins and that Pa served in the Confederate army in the war.

Squirrel Huntin' Sam is a nephew of Pa's and the best hunter of squirrels in these mountains. But he's teched in the head. I ought to know. He was still in the sixth grade when I started school. For the third year. At recess he'd catch birds and kill them, just for the fun of watching them die. I could have told them about Squirrel Huntin' Sam, if they'd asked me. But nobody ever does ask me much of anything, even now. When you're the youngest, you stay the youngest forever.

It was fall. Hunting season. Which is almost a religious holiday in these mountains. The crops were laid by and the men were off. From our place, through the autumn woods, you could hear the sounds of the hunt: squirrels and partridges rushing to take cover, the braying of the dogs, the calling of the horn, and then the distant report of the guns going off. It was exciting and scary at the same time. I love the woods as much as the next person, but I always knew that hunting time was a time of death, that it had a dark side to it that meant the ending of things.

It was the ending of things for Bill Staton, who was half Hatfield and had sworn at the pig trial that he'd seen Floyd mark those creatures as his own. Squirrel Huntin' Sam had taunted him for a lying traitor after that, and Staton saw his chance to get even.

He shot Paris McCoy, Sam's brother, who was out hunting with him. Sam fought Staton and killed him. Paris recovered, but Sam was taken to Logan Jail in West Virginia to be held for trial.

Before you knew it, there was Pa, his gun at the ready, saying they had to get Sam out of jail. Most of the time Pa wouldn't even admit to kinship with Sam. But a McCoy was a McCoy. And a McCoy in a West Virginia jail was like a chicken in the jaws of a fox. Pa rallied his kin. A hundred of them went to the trial. But Sam was freed, and he's still floating around out in those woods, disgusting as ever, killing things for the fun of it.

That's the big story about Pa's sow and pigs, which means nothing to me. I don't care how much they all say the trouble started with that.

It would have sat there, that trouble, and never festered, never started up again, if not for my sister Roseanna. And I can say this, because I loved her best of all.

Chapter Three

1880

ROSEANNA AND I had little iron bedsteads in our room in the house on Blackberry Fork. They were covered with quilts Mama made. And we had calico curtains on the windows, too. It was a real nice room. Roseanna made it nice. She had a looking glass over a little wooden dressing table that brother Floyd made for her. "Like grand ladies do," she told me. I don't know how Ro knew what grand ladies did, but I took her word for it. She let me use the little dressing table and taught me how to curl up my hair in rags. And she let me touch all her things, like the brooch Pa gave her when she turned twenty-one that belonged to his very own mama. Even the combs she put in her hair, her good embroidered handkerchiefs, and her scented soap. She made that soap herself. When we cooked up a batch, she took some aside and put some decoction in it that made it smell good. Adelaide called it her witch's brew. I knew for a fact that the scent came from some little heart-shaped leaves in the woods. But I didn't tell anybody. I know how to keep a secret.

Roseanna could always make a silk purse out of a sow's ear, that's what Mama said. I thought Roseanna could do miracles. I depended on her for it.

Adelaide, Alifair, and Trinvilla shared a bigger room, but they could have it. I was never allowed in there. They had their secret things. Alifair made corncob dolls that were precious to her. And Trinvilla had her box of dye recipes. I didn't care about any of it, not even Adelaide's herbs. She was only ten to my seven when the trouble with Roseanna started but already coming on to be a little old granny woman. Mama let her visit with Aunt Cory, a real granny woman, and stay for days. I think Adelaide did it just to get out of chores.

Adelaide and Trinvilla were jealous of Ro because she was so purty and all the boys in Pike County wanted to court her. And they were hateful to me because I was Ro's pet. They were all the time whispering how she was going to come to perdition. But Adelaide and Trinvilla didn't even know what perdition was. And didn't care. If Alifair said Ro was going to come to it, they agreed. They'd agree with anything she said. I think they had a quarter of a brain between them.

Truth to tell, I didn't know the meaning of the word, either. But I learned it on Election Day, 1880. The day Ro ran off.

THE NIGHT BEFORE Election Day was the first time I saw Yeller Thing. I was out back by the corncrib, stuffing straw in mattress tickings. The mattresses had to be filled with clean straw every fall. Adelaide was supposed to be helping me, but she'd wandered off to get some ginseng down in the holler by the briar thickets. So I wandered off, too, across the creek to the woods to check on my playhouse and get my dolly that Floyd had carved me.

The sun was all but down and the woods were filled with shadows and the sounds birds make when they're going to sleep. I fetched my doll, climbed down the ladder, and then I heard the noise, the rustling nearby. At first I thought it was Adelaide, come to spy on me, because I never allowed her in my playhouse. But nobody was there. Again the rustling, this time closer, and I got scairt. Just off a piece, across the holler, I could see our house, all solid and snuggly, with smoke coming out of the chimney. How could anything hurt me so close to our house?

But I knew better. Hadn't Calvin warned me about snakes, and even bears? I searched the ground around me, peered into the blue shadows. The sun was gone, it was coming on to night. The woods were no place for a little girl at night. I turned to go, then heard it again, the rustling.

Before I turned I smelled it. And almost laughed. A skunk! I turned to see where it was and that is when I saw Yeller Thing for the first time.

It whooshed past me. I almost felt the draft it made. And the smell got worse than anything, even worse than the outhouse at school in September.

I know what I saw. It was yeller. And big. Bigger than anything in these woods had a right to be, even a bear. It streaked by like a painter cat. And there was this eerie sound. Not a growl. It sounded like a Rebel yell, from what my pa told me about such yells. Or like a man about to die, which is maybe the same thing.

For a moment I stood stock-still. And then I heard the words Mama so often read from her Bible: "And it is appointed unto men once to die."

Those words just came into my head. And I knew then that what was out there was nothing animal or human. The knowing flooded through me, and I ran. Back through the holler, across the creek, and up to our house, through the back door, yelling, "Mama, Mama, I saw the Devil!"

Mama calmed me. She gave me cookies and warm milk. And she scolded, too.

"If you'd paid mind to your chores and finished filling that mattress ticking, you wouldn't be in trouble. Where's Adelaide?"

I sipped my warm milk, still shivering. "Out picking ginseng."

I saw Mama look across the kitchen at Floyd, who was sipping some coffee at the table. My brother Floyd is old. Twenty-eight at least. He has his own little log cabin a piece away from us, on the creek, where he makes his moonshine and his toys. He travels around selling those toys every fall and sells the moonshine all the year round. He is not so all-fired-up taken with Pa as the others are. Floyd is different. Alifair said he has girls wherever he goes selling his toys. But he never speaks about them. Every once in a while he comes to sup with us.

"Go find Adelaide," Mama said to Floyd.

Floyd got right to his feet. "Where's she picking?" he asked me. He had Pa's long gun in his hand.

"Down in the holler by the briar thickets."

He made for the door.

"He won't be after Adelaide," I told him. "He's come for me."

Floyd looked at me with those steel gray eyes of his. He's a quiet sort, but nice. Lots of times I go to visit him at his cabin and bring him some hot biscuits or fresh preserved jam. He lets me touch the toys he's making, the jumping jack, the little farm sled. He asks my opinion about girls' toys. And listens to what I tell him.

"Why's he come for you?" he asked. And I knew he believed me.

"He's come to tell me something. To warn me." The words were out of my mouth before I knew it. But they were right sounding. "But I don't know about what."

Floyd nodded. He understood. When people hereabouts tell stories of haints, others don't disbelieve. Some tell of seeing ghosts of tormented souls. Some of witches come to make your soul tormented.

"Best put a drop of turpentine and some sugar in that milk of hers," he told Mama. Then he went out the door.

I know what that's for, a fretful little 'un. It'll make them sleep. Oh, how I hate being the youngest! Mama did as Floyd said, then made me wash and go right to bed.

Chapter Four

1880

THE NEXT DAY was bright with sun and bursting like a hog bladder with the excitement of the elections. I went early with Roseanna. She smelled so sweet and looked so purty in her new calico. Her hair was all curled and shiny. Because I'd fallen asleep early, she couldn't do my hair up in rags, so she fixed it in one long braid down my back and put a sassy ribbon on it.

When we got to the schoolhouse, the menfolk were already there, all done up in their best, standing around and joking in little groups, and they stopped all that jawing and stared at Ro when we walked up. I could have busted with pride. Even Ambrose Cuzlin, my teacher, who was standing by the schoolhouse door welcoming everybody, had a grin for Roseanna.

Everybody was there. One glance around told you that. Republicans and Democrats, young men and old, the well-placed and the dirt-poor, Hatfields and McCoys.

Ro and I sort of stayed off to ourselves for a while, under a locust tree. Nobody bothered her outright, because my brothers were there, all of them, and that's quite a parcel.

Floyd had brought his moonshine, of course. Tolbert came with his wife and baby. Brother James was there with his family. They live a mile below us on Pond Creek. James has five children already and is older than Floyd even. James is a deputy sheriff and everybody knows he doesn't pussyfoot around the law but is a man to be reckoned with.

Brother Sam was there with his Martha, too. They live on Dials Fork. Bill, who was twelve, was with Bud, who was just sixteen and coming on to be a man. Calvin was eighteen, and already one. Pharmer was fifteen, brave, handsome, and good already with a gun. I've got a brother Lilburn, in his twenties, but he's off somewhere looking for gold. Lordy, I could have left somebody out. When it comes to my family, I never know.

Alifair, Adelaide, and Trinvilla were coming later with Mama.

All the boys gave me and Roseanna their howdy, then walked off to be with their friends. It seemed so funny to see all those people walking in our schoolhouse, and I was more than just a mite glad that Mr. Cuzlin had made us neaten it good. He was proud of that log schoolhouse. All by himself he put backs on the puncheon seats.

There was lots of shouting and insulting and slapping on the back the way men do to each other. The women-folk were gathered under the trees in their Sunday best, setting down baskets of food and spreading cloths on the tables. Everybody brought food, even the young girls. Not Roseanna. She brought herself. It was enough, and everybody knew it. Children ran back and forth playing tag and crack-the-whip. Some of the smaller boys from school had squirt guns.

I saw Nancy McCoy. She was fifteen and still in school with us. She's Uncle Harmon's youngest, spoiled and fussed over by her big brothers because her pa was killed before she was born. She thought she was the purtiest girl on Peter Creek. Well, she couldn't hold a candle to Ro, even though the boys all moon like sick calves over her at school, including the younger ones. If you want to talk about perdition, she was headed for it all right.

Onliest one who wasn't there was Belle Beaver. She lived in a little lean-to in Happy Holler. She was a fancy woman. Alifair, who thinks she knows everything, said Belle was whipped out of North Carolina, so she came here. But women didn't want her around and had already gone in a delegation to my brother Jim to see about running her out. So far Jim hadn't said he would and hadn't said he wouldn't.

Me, Adelaide, and Trinvilla walk by Happy Holler on our way to school. Adelaide and Trinvilla really run by, afeared of seeing Belle. I think Alifair told them that she can taint them with her evil ways. I know she can't, because Ma sends me two or three times a year with baskets of vittles. I've never been in her shanty, but she's always been nice to me. I'm not afeared of her.

Everything was going on the way it should, with the men voting and feeling good about themselves and everybody gathering around to eat and catching up on things. You couldn't help but notice that the McCoys stayed on their own patch of ground and the Hatfields staked out another. Most of the Hatfields came over from West Virginia, so they couldn't vote. They came just to find out what was going on. There was some calling back and forth. Some howdies, and lots of long looks, but no trouble. Not until young Johnse Hatfield started walking in our direction.

My brother Bill had already started playing his fiddle. I was listening to that sweet but mournful sound behind all the talk and laughter when I looked up and saw Johnse coming toward us. "Ro," I said.

She'd have died before she let on she knew he was coming. She was sitting there making a cornhusk doll for me and calling something over to Nancy McCoy about her dress. But she knew Johnse was coming. Every pore of her knew it.

"Pa will kill us, Ro." Hatfields and McCoys never spoke to each other. If we broke that rule here, every man would have his hand on his gun quicker than you could say moonshine.

Yet here was Johnse Hatfield walking toward us.

"Howdy there, girls." And he leaned against that locust tree, grinning for all he was worth.

I could have thought a lot of things in that moment.

But the first thing that came to my mind was how I'd learned in school about the Minute Men in Lexington up north and how they stood and faced the British soldiers. "Then someone fired a shot," my teacher, Mr. Cuzlin, told us. "And it was the shot heard round the world."

That's what Johnse Hatfield's howdy was that day to us. The shot heard all through West Virginia and Kentucky. I may have been only seven, but I knew that much, anyways.

———

DID THE TALK and laughter all around us stop? Did the people look, without turning? Did they hear without trying? Did the birds stop singing and the whole world tilt just an itty-bitty bit? I felt it. All of it. But nothing else mattered, because though Ro hadn't yet favored him with a howdy, or even a look, my eyes filled up with Johnse Hatfield.

I knew what Pa told us about Hatfields better than I knew my Bible lessons. *The waters saw thee, Oh God, the waters saw thee and were afraid: the depths also were troubled.*

Was Psalm 77 about God? Or the Hatfields? Could it be about Johnse Hatfield? Teeth so white, smile so sassy, eyes so blue? And dimples! What was it Ma said about dimples? "Sometimes you don't know if the Lord poked His finger there or the Devil." With Johnse I was sure it was the Devil. He moved like a painter cat. He smelled like my brothers, of strong soap, tobacco, corn liquor, and horses. But oh, I never felt like that around my brothers. So then, why was my soul troubled? And me only seven! Think what Ro was feeling! I looked up at him worshipfully.

My sister tossed her head but still didn't look. Kept on with that doll like her life depended on it. "Hello yourself. You're takin' quite a chance coming over here like this, aren't you?"

"I figure you're worth it."

"Do you now?"

"Sure 'nuf." Still with that insolent grin. Still leaning against the locust tree. "You got a feller, Roseanna McCoy?"

"Nope. But I can't see what business it is of yourn."

"I could make it my business if'n you gave me the chance."

She was still sitting there working on that doll. "And how do you plan to do that, with my pa and brothers and fifty other McCoys all around us like bees around honey?"

"You got the honey part right," Johnse said. "Why don't you leave the bees to me? I kin handle 'em."

"I'd like to know how, is what I'd like to know."

"Heck." And Johnse moved from the tree, a little more toward her. "They're all so fired up on corn liquor and politics nobody'd even notice if'n we sashayed down to that bunch of trees over there by the creek where it's cool. Nobody'd even miss us."

"You think that, do you?" my sister asked.

"I know it. I'd bet my life on it."

Roseanna finished with the doll and handed it to me. "There you go, baby. You wait here. I'll be right back." Then she got up, smoothed her skirt, and still without looking at Johnse, they walked together away from the locust tree and down to the creek.

The waters of the creek will see thee, Johnse Hatfield, they will see thee and also be troubled.

I waited. She didn't come right back. I got a plate of food and went to wait under the locust tree with my cornhusk doll. I'd wait all day if Roseanna wanted. But she just didn't come.

Chapter Five

1880

SOMETHING HAD HAPPENED and I didn't know what. Where had Ro gone? One part of me didn't think it was right of her to do me like that, and the other was loyal as a bee worker to its queen. If only I knew what had happened!

Had Ro and Johnse meant what they said to each other, or was it in some kind of code that I wasn't privy to because I was just a little 'un? Always I was just a little 'un. When would I be big enough to understand?

I understood this much. Ro would never go off with a Hatfield. She was going to do some terrible thing to him down there by the creek. She'd come back laughing and all my brothers would crowd around and tell her she'd done good.

She didn't come back. And from then on it seemed that nobody in our family laughed ever again. Not for the right reasons, anyways.

THE SUN WAS slanting on the other side of that locust tree and the shadows deepening when Pa came over to me. "Fanny, where's your sister?"

"She went for a walk down by the creek." If you lie to Pa you lie to God. I knew that since I was just a knee baby. But my heart and soul belonged not to Pa then. Or even to God. But to Ro.

He looked in that direction, and I held my breath. "We'll be a-startin' home soon. Go tell her."

I got up. "Yes, Pa."

Then someone called him and he walked back to his friends.

I'd missed the game of Fox and Geese. I'd missed Kitty Walks a Corner, too. And the puppet show Mr. Cuzlin put on with puppets made by my brother Floyd. I'd wanted to watch the boys play Town Ball. My brother Bud was playing. No matter. I went to find Ro.

I had to walk across the creek, so I unbuttoned and took off my shoes and hose. The water was cool. "Ro!" I called. "Ro, where are you?"

Why did I call? Because I wanted to give her warning I was a-comin' is why. Because I suppose that I knew all the while that she was not throwing Johnse into the creek. I knew they had other more interesting things to do. Else why would they be hiding over there in the thicket like they were?

"Here, Fanny."

Her blouse was drooping off one shoulder. Her hair was mussed. Her shoes were off and Johnse's shirt was all the way unbuttoned in front. Alifair would say she should be whipped out o' Kentucky if she saw her. She held out her arms to me. "Here I am, baby. Come here."

I went to her. "Pa says we're to go home soon."

Johnse was buttoning his shirt.

"Good. You go on home with Pa. Did you have a nice time today, Fanny?"

"No. I waited for you and you didn't come."

"Well, I had things to do."

"What things?"

"I had to talk to Johnse. About important things." She knelt down in front of me then, and I saw something in her face and her eyes I'd never seen before. Some happiness, like she knew a secret.

"You're not coming?"

"No, Fanny baby."

I didn't like the way she said Fanny baby. Something was not right here. She was pleading for my understanding. How could I give it to her when I didn't understand? "Where you going, Ro?" But I think I already knew.

"Home with Johnse. He's asked to me to marry him."

Ma has a saying: "God doesn't give us a burden heavier than we can handle." *Well maybe not,* I thought, standing there, *but our families sure do.* "Marry?"

She gave a little laugh. "Sure. Don't you think it's time I got married, Fanny? Mr. Hatfield will give us some land and we'll have a cabin built. And you can come see us, just like you visit Tolbert and Mary."

"You been drinking corn liquor, Ro? You can't marry him," I whispered. "Pa will kill you. And him."

She laughed. "I'm not afraid of Pa."

How could she not be? When Pa got riled up it was terrible, worse than what the preacher told us God was like when he threw Adam and Eve out of Paradise. But that was why I looked up to her so, because she lived outside the circle of Pa's anger and Ma's religion. A place I wanted to live. It was why Alifair hated her. Still there was something plumb daft about it. Like she'd been bewitched. She'd seen Yeller Thing maybe and he'd turned her head. But then I looked up at Johnse and I thought no. She'd only seen Johnse Hatfield. But it was enough.

"I'm twenty-one, Fanny," she said. "I'm of age."

I felt a catch in my throat, a heaviness in my chest. And there came a rustling of wind then, like before rain. I looked up. The dark was coming because Ro was going. The light I'd known was pouring out of me, like my life's blood, and leaving me dark. "If you marry him you'll be a Hatfield," I said. It was all I could think of to say.

"That's all foolishness now, and you know it. All this fussing between our two families. Johnse and I have been studying on it all afternoon here. We figure if we marry it'll end all the hate between our two families. Ain't that right, Johnse?"

"Sure will," he said. "We both mean too much to our kin for them to disown us."

"So you go on back to Pa." She stood up, still smiling. "Go on. Once we're wed there ain't a thing he kin do about it."

I turned to go. "What'll I say?"

"Nothing, honey. You don't say a word. Tell Pa you couldn't find me. When we're wed we'll let them know, sure 'nuf."

"That's a lie, Ro."

"Only a teenie little one. God won't mind."

"Ma will. She'll put my pebble on the damned side of her tree stump."

"Fanny baby, you couldn't be damned. I don't care where Ma puts your pebble."

I was near to crying. But I turned and started back. The wind was really kicking up now, turning the tree leaves so you could see the silver under them. It was even starting to rain. I could see back to the clearing by the schoolhouse. People were gathering things up, women putting on shawls, families making for their wagons.

"Hurry," Ro urged. "Go on now. Run."

I turned again. "I always wanted to be at your wedding, Roseanna," I said.

"I know. But things don't always work out how we plan. Tell you what, you kin put some of my glycerin and rosewater on tonight afore you go to bed."

I was always begging for some and she would never give it. But my heart just got heavier as it came to me what all this meant. Ro wouldn't be in our room with me anymore. The bed next to me would be empty. She'd be sleeping tonight with Johnse Hatfield!

I ran. Rain was coming down heavier. I didn't even stop to put on my hose and boots. I just ran to where I saw Ma and Pa. And when Pa asked, "Where's Ro?" I said I couldn't find her.

"She must have walked on ahead," Ma said. I got into the wagon and she wrapped her shawl around me. Alifair was staring at me like she knew something. I looked away. The thought of living at home under Alifair's ways, without Ro, sickened me.

"Don't know why Ro can go her way, and we always have to come when you call, Ma," Alifair said. But Ma only told her to hush and started humming "If Everybody Was Like Jesus What a Wonderful World This Would Be."

Thunder rolled overhead. Lightning lit up the sky. I thought of Ro and Johnse. Where would they find a preacher tonight? Were preacher men ready to read vows over young folk any time of the day or night in West Virginia? Because that's where Ro would bed down tonight. In West Virginia. Across the Tug Branch of the Big Sandy River.

Pa had the reins, and my brother Bud held his rifle at the ready as we drove through the woods. I looked for Yeller Thing, but I never saw him at all.

Chapter Six

1880

THERE WERE NINE of us children still living home at the time and I can close my eyes today and see us as we all sat around the kitchen table that night after the elections.

I want that night back with all of us together having tea. Even if Alifair made it and considered herself in charge of the kitchen. That's what she always wanted, to be the woman of the house. Like Tolbert says, she should have her own place.

But I'd even take Alifair's sass if it meant I could go back to that night and hear Pa and the boys talking about Mr. Buggin's crops or the new springhouse Mr. Taylor was making. And Trinvilla saying how Mr. Randolph was going to start buying ginseng, witch-hazel leaves, yellowroot, poke, and cherry bark to sell in his general store.

I should tell about our house, now. It's important.

It was a big house, our place on Blackberry Fork. I don't want anybody who happens to read this to think that just because it was a log cabin it was an old poke of a place with a dirt floor. Pa built it soon's he came out of Virginia and married Ma in 1849. I have to give the Devil his due. It was a right fine house Pa built.

The kitchen first, because that's where we all gathered, where Pa held forth when he chose to lecture, scold, or instruct, where we said prayers before bedtime, led by Mama. There was a big round table in the middle and chairs. Oak. The cupboard that held all Ma's dishes was oak, too. Then there was the washbasin set on a table with a bucket of water under it. We washed dishes in a big old tub that sat near the washbasin. Pa had put in a hollow bamboo cane to drain the water outside. In the corner was Ma's wood range that she always kept blackened just right, the one with the warming closets on top that I miss so now. Adelaide and I had a stool we'd use to reach them. Anytime of the day you could reach in there and get biscuits and they were always warm. And there'd be a pot of soup boiling on the new of the moon. Because that's when it jelled best.

Over the kitchen was a hanging whale-oil lamp, given to Ma by her father when she wed. Ma didn't trust it, purty as it was with flowers painted on it. She'd rather burn candles. Said that oil lamp would burn just right when we were alone, but as soon as the preacher or somebody important came to call it would smoke and the oil would run over. Ma said there was no end to the wickedness that lamp would do to embarrass her. I wondered if it didn't have to do with the fact that her father never wanted her to wed Pa in the first place.

So we used candles. Some families in town had kerosene. But Ma said it was the Devil's own decoction, that people who used it had a covenant with him. Downstairs, too, we had the parlor where the spinning wheel and a loom sat. There were the horns from the first deer my brother Bud shot, an old piano somebody gave Pa when he saved a man's horse from dying, stuffed thatched rockers, a picture of Pa in his uniform from the war, our family Bible, and a shelf of books: *Pilgrim's Progress, Notes on the State of Virginia, Tristram Shandy, The Deerslayer, The Scarlet Letter,* and *The Rime of the Ancient Mariner.*

You may think they were high-toned for people plain as us. Unless you knew that they were loaned to my brother Calvin by Mr. Ambrose Cuzlin. Calvin was eighteen then, but he still attended our school when he could. It only goes to eighth grade, but Mr. Cuzlin let him keep coming because he said Calvin had a mournful need to learn. Only a month before that election day Calvin gave a speech on good government at the Fourth of July celebration. Pa said Mr. Cuzlin was giving Calvin notions, but as long as he did his chores Pa let him go.

Upstairs were our bedrooms—four. Ma and Pa had the second to biggest with an old rope bed that Pa had put slats in, a washstand and a clock, and rag rugs on the floor. Nice curtains, too—calico.

Down the hall was the biggest room. The boys' room, where Bill, Bud, Pharmer, and Calvin slept. Four beds, solid oak with the headboards decorated with birds and animals burned in by my brother Floyd, four wash-basins where they shaved their faces every morning. Where Bill tried to shave every morning, even though he only had fuzz, at fourteen.

The room for Trinvilla, Adelaide, and Alifair was across from mine and Ro's. We took the smaller room so we could be together.

In front of our house there was an early spring garden. Pa said they used to call 'em kitchen gardens. It was just where the porch ended and it got the morning sun. The smokehouse was in back and so were the bigger gardens. That's where the pole beans were, where Pa and the boys grew cabbages, potatoes, carrots, tomatoes, squash, onions, corn, and beets. The barn was up the incline behind the house. And there was a little house a bit aways from ours. That's where Faithful Black Mookie once lived. Tolbert told me that Faithful Black Mookie was a slave Ma and Pa had before the war. But he was misnamed, because he ran away while Pa was off fighting. James, Tolbert, Floyd, and Sam remember him. We used that little house for storage, and every so often, if Ma sent me in to fetch something, I could feel the haint of Faithful Black Mookie there. Like he never left.

His old quilt was still in the corner, ragged and damp. So was his shirt, on a peg on the wall. Why did he leave without his shirt? I wonder. But think! Us with a slave! And some of my brothers old enough to recollect him!

The well was out back, behind the kitchen, and it was a hundred feet deep. Every once in a while me and Bill would pull the big piece of slate off it and peer down into the dark depths. We'd drop a pebble in, wait, and hear it plop.

The cellar was near as important as the kitchen. Pa and my older brothers had made a ring of big rocks right in the middle for a fire and put in a clay pipe that somehow drew the smoke out. That's where we did the wash, not down by the river like some families. That's where we made hominy, where Ma cooked her lard. And there we had whole sections of chestnut logs hollowed out to store meat in after it was cured. And holes dug in the ground for our vegetables we wanted to keep through the winter.

I just don't want anybody to think we were squatters, or dirt farmers or anything, because we weren't. My brother Pharmer kept bees, Bud hunted, Calvin traded horses. We all had our place. And when I think of us now as we were that night when we got home from elections, I know that even though Ro wasn't there it was one of the last close times we had as a family.

Ro was missed. But nobody said anything about her not coming home. That was Ma and Pa's business.

Of course, Alifair questioned me, in private. "Did she say where she was going?" I lied and said no. I was already grieving for Ro's leaving, but there was also this little tingly excitement in me because she was going to get married. And I was the only one who knew it.

I'd give all I am to go back to the way it was when we were together, all of a piece. I want to go back so bad I'd let myself be dragged through the woods forever by Yeller Thing, made part of his terror, to have it back for just one night.

But God doesn't work it that way. How could He? Why He can scarce keep track of things now. How would it be with everybody asking Him, "God, I want to go back and do it over"? He gives us one chance, that's all. And fools that we are, we never get it right.

Chapter Seven

1880

THE ROOM WAS so lonely without Ro. I felt like I'd fallen into a gopher hole. I lay in my bed and stared into the darkness as I listened to the sounds of the household settling into bed. At one time I felt so pitiful lost I got out of bed and started toward Ma and Pa's room. From the other side of the door I heard them talking. It was about Ro. I stood and listened.

They were conjecturing where she could be. I heard Ma say might be she'd gone to Aunt Betty's, but she never went off before without telling.

Pa said she was of age and she had sense.

Ma said Alifair was of age, too, but never stayed away of a night except when she went to revival meetings. Ma was afeared, she said.

Pa said Ro might be the purtiest girl in three counties but push comes to shove she could put a bear in his place.

Ma said it weren't bears she was worried about. It was the way some of the boys were a-lookin' at Ro today that put the righteous fear of the Lord into her.

Pa said, all right, all right, after this day he'd talk to Ro about not staying out without first telling where she was fixing to stay. He said if she didn't come home by morning he'd have the boys go out and ask around.

Then Ma said, why did the Lord try her like that, giving her the purtiest girl in three counties? Why couldn't she be plain like the others?

It hurt me that Ma thought me, Adelaide, Trinvilla, and Alifair plain, but I was used to it. Ro was always spoke of as the purtiest.

Pa answered it was because the Lord couldn't help Himself. Ro just took right after her ma in looks. Everything got quiet then, so I went back to my room. I tried not to look in the direction of Ro's bed.

I wasn't guilty anymore about not telling them what I knew after Ma said that. All I could think was, *Is Ro married yet?* How could she be married when she didn't even have a quilt? A girl had to have at least three quilts before she could wed. And Ro had never gotten around to starting hers. I wished I wasn't so little. I'd make her one. I was learning to piece a quilt, just doing the running stitch. I wondered if Ro wouldn't like a nice bearpaw pattern.

I lay awake a long time. I heard a hooty owl call, then a nightbird. Heard Old Blue, my brother Bud's hunting dog, howling outside. Soon he was joined by Old Rags, Bill's dog. Then all I heard was the locusts, then wind rustling the trees.

Suppose they couldn't find a preacher in West Virginia this time of night. Would Devil Anse let them in? Mama once said that a person who let people who weren't wed stay at their house overnight kept a bad house. Well, old Devil Anse's house was bad anyways.

Almost soon's I fell asleep, it seemed, somebody was shaking me. "Fanny! Get up!" Alifair, sure 'nuf. "You come on now. Up, or you don't get any vittles I cook in this house."

I sat up and rubbed my eyes. "I didn't hardly sleep."

"Neither did anybody else, thanks to your wonderful Ro. Come on now, lazy girl. Up."

My brothers, rifles in hand, were near out the door when I got down. Pa was bellowing, "I want every friend and relative questioned if'n you don't see her on the road comin' home."

I heard a whimper from Ma. Alifair thumped the buttermilk pitcher down on the table and glared at me. "You were with her. Where did she go?"

Brilliant sunshine spilled into the kitchen and hurt my eyes. I was hungry. I reached for some ham, but Alifair clamped her hand down on my wrist. "She knows something, Pa."

Everybody stopped to look at me. I felt Pa's gaze fixed on me. His eyes were brown, but now they looked like blackstrap molasses. "Fanny, where's your sister?"

"I don't know, Pa. Like I told you yesterday, last I saw her she took a walk to the creek."

If you lie to Pa you lie to God. But I kept at it, throwing my lies right in God's face, hoping he wouldn't punish me by making something terrible happen to Roseanna.

"Did you go tell her we were leaving yesterday like I asked?"

"I couldn't find her, Pa. Then it started to rain and I come running."

I knew I'd be punished real bad if they found out I was lying.

"Alifair, let your sister at the ham," Pa ordered.

I let myself breathe again. They believed me! Ma and Pa and my brothers, leastways. Even Adelaide and Trinvilla, though I knew Alifair would soon bring them around to what she was thinking. Which was that I was lying my eyes out and I'd rot in hellfire for it.

My brothers left. Pa sat down to finish his breakfast with the rest of us. They spoke no more of Ro, but I found then that I could scarce eat, hungry as I was. Because every time I looked at her empty chair I felt sick inside. Ro would likely never sit at this table with us again. Terror gripped me as I thought that I might never see my sister Ro again, either.

———

ALIFAIR HAD CLEAR blue eyes and glossy brown-red hair that she wore pulled back. Her face was always scrubbed clean as was everything about her person. And that's how she was. Clean. No wiles. No head tossing. No lowering of the eyelashes. Alifair was so honest it hurt. Her words went right in your face, and if you didn't like them, you could go skin a skunk.

Sometimes I wished she'd like me. But she didn't, and there was nothing for it.

She milked the cows. It was her idea, not Pa's. She wanted to be in charge of those cows as much as she wanted to be in charge of the house. She knew when to turn 'em out and when to keep 'em in the barn. She kept the milk crocks clean and churned the butter. She fed the cows corn nubbins, fodder, shucks, and tops. She'd go with Pa, twice a year, down to cotton country to get cottonseed for 'em. It was the only time she stayed away except for healing or revival meetings.

"I want you to come out to the barn with me," she said as I sat finishing my breakfast.

I knew what was coming. But I sassed her anyways, remembering what brother Tolbert had said. "Isn't there a revival meeting coming up soon?" I asked.

She stopped what she was doing and pulled me out of the chair and dragged me out to the barn with her. To see the new calf, she told Ma. There was no new calf. There was me, whipped up the ladder to the hayloft with a switch on my legs, and made to stay there while she cleaned the cow stalls. Or for as long as she wanted. Until I told her the truth about Ro.

———

I DIDN'T TELL. Along about noon my brothers came back with the news that everybody they'd talked to said Ro had gone off yesterday with Johnse Hatfield.

Since Calvin, at eighteen, was the oldest at home, he

48

told it in the kitchen. "John Hatfield said he saw her crossing the Tug with Devil Anse's boy, Johnse, yester evenin'."

I saw Pa's face blacken. Heard Ma's gasp. "John is half McCoy," Pa allowed. "He can be trusted."

"But why?" Ma asked. "Where was she a-goin' with Johnse?" Ma looked like she'd just swallowed some boiled onions in molasses for a sore throat.

"Where do you think?" Pa asked. "She's been taken by the son of that Devil Anse Hatfield. Likely she's run off to wed. But far as I'm concerned, she's lost all notions of respectability. She has forsaken us, everything we stand for. I don't hold with such. So far as I'm concerned, we forget Roseanna. Her name has gone from this house. She no more crosses my threshold."

Again Ma gasped. "Pa, aren't you being a little unforgiving?"

He looked at her. "Roseanna—and this is the last time I'll say her name—knew what she was a-doin'. She set out to hurt us, trafficking with a Hatfield. I tell you, she's gone from this house!"

"Alifair," Ma said, "strip Roseanna's bed. Burn the linens. Fanny, go put her pebble on the side of the damned."

I stood rooted to the floor. I could not believe all this. It was a bad dream. Just yestermorn me and Ro had set off with our family's blessing to the elections, laughter from the house echoing in our ears, Ma calling after us to make sure we had our shawls. Now I would never see my sister Ro again.

I felt a big fist inside me, squeezing my heart. Then I felt Alifair's glare. "Go," she whispered. "Do as Ma says." She grabbed my arm and smacked my bottom. I ran out the door sobbing to put Ro's pebble on the side of the damned.

Chapter Eight

1880

A MONTH WENT by. A month of heat and locusts. Of chores and church and no Roseanna. Me alone in the room, looking at her stripped bed, her things setting there in the corner in a burlap bag, as Pa had decreed they be. A month of Alifair herding me around, bossing me, and knowing there was no Ro to take my part. Alifair wanted to move into my room to "take charge" of me, she told Ma. I told Ma I'd die first. I begged her not to allow it, so she didn't. "We'll wait a bit," she told Alifair. "Ro may be back." It was part of the world Ma lived in that made her believe this.

"Why would she be back if'n she's wed?" Alifair asked. Usually she let Ma live in her world. Because that's what gave her leave to take over the kitchen. Now she wasn't about to.

"Maybe she isn't," Ma answered.

"Well, if she isn't then she's living in sin. And Pa won't let her back."

Ma didn't answer and Alifair didn't move in. Ma was still woman of the house after all.

The sheep came home and left again. Ma made me, Trinvilla, and Adelaide new dresses for school. Nights got cool and there was a ring around the full moon. I went to my playhouse a lot and saw that the muskrats had built their houses big and the north side of the beaver dam on the creek was more covered with sticks than the south side. All signs of a bad winter.

Pa and my brothers started gathering in the crops. We planted fall turnips and cabbages. They pushed over the collards and put pine bark and dirt over them to keep 'em for the winter. We stored the pumpkins in the shuck pen, the sweet potatoes in the smokehouse. My brothers cut and stacked wood. We made a batch of soap from the hickory and oak ashes. I started school.

From the first day there were strange looks and whisperings. I knew the other kids were talking about Ro. I kept my nose to my primer and stayed to myself. Adelaide and Trinvilla told Alifair how embarrassed they were that Ro was now common gossip. She told them that's what happened when you came to perdition and they should just learn from it.

One especially chilly September morning Ma sent me with a basket to Belle Beaver's shack. Adelaide and Trinvilla teased me about it all the way, and shouted "ask her about Ro" when they continued on to school as I stopped.

Belle came to the door, all wrapped in something silk that didn't go with her surroundings and made you think of far-off places. She wasn't a bit embarrassed. "Thank that nice mama of yours," she said. "She's a true Christian."

I said I would. Her hair was some color I'd never seen. She had rouge on her cheeks. Was this what happened when a person came to perdition? Would Ro look like this someday?

"Heard your sister wed that nice Johnse Hatfield," she said. "And they're all carryin' on like she run off with some Yankee. I know what it is to be vilified. You wait here." And while I stood there wondering what *vilified* meant, she disappeared into her shack and in a little bit came out with a hair comb. "Give this to her. She'll like it, bein' new wed and all."

I was so touched by her gift that I took it, mumbled my thanks, and went on my way. What a beautiful comb! But I couldn't give it to Ro. It would make her vilified, like Belle. I threw it in the woods on my way to school, mourning the loss of its purtiness. I'd probably never see another like it.

At recess I was out at the pump fetching some water for Mr. Cuzlin when out comes Nancy McCoy, all gussied up in her new calico. Pink it was, and with her dark curls she looked right purty in it. Most girls were through with school by Nancy's age and were home helping out. But Nancy kept right on coming, when she pleased. And it wasn't like Calvin, who wanted to learn. Nancy came because she had nothing else to do. And she was always making sheep eyes, either at Mr. Cuzlin or Calvin. Both paid her no nevermind.

She was carrying a green peach-tree stick, forked at the end. "You want to see me find water?" she asked. "I can find water with this. I'm doing an experiment."

I went right on pumping. "Got all the water I need."

She stopped to look at me. "Bet I could find your sister for you, too."

I went right on pumping. "What do you know about Ro?"

"She's living with Johnse Hatfield. At Devil Anse's house. And they ain't married."

My face flamed. "Not true."

"It is so. My brother Lark told me. And he knows."

I finished filling my bucket with water, and we stood there staring at each other. "Living without benefit of marriage," Nancy whispered. "Lark has friends in West Virginny. And he knows. And soon so will everybody. You see? I told you I could find your sister for you with my peach stick, didn't I?"

I took the peach stick from her and broke it in two. "Liar!"

"That's no way to treat kin," she said gravely.

"Don't care if you're kin. You're a liar!" I threw the water at her. It went all over her new pink calico. I dropped the bucket and ran. Not back to the schoolhouse, but home. All the way, crying. And who was there in the yard? Alifair. Demanding to know why I was home. I wouldn't tell her, of course. I couldn't. And that's when she put my head under the pump, trying to make me tell, and Ma came out and stopped her and packed my bag and sent me to Tolbert and Mary's.

———

SO I WASN'T there at supper when my family got the news that Ro and Johnse weren't wed. Bad news travels faster than a brushfire in these parts. I was just setting down to supper with Tolbert, Mary, and little Cora, my hair still wet, when Calvin rode up and came in to tell us.

"Pa found out that Ro's been at Devil Anse's all this time with Johnse. Not wed." Calvin spoke the words without feeling and accepted a dish of food from Mary. "Pa's all fit to be tied. It's the first time he spoke her name since she left, and I wish he hadn't."

Tolbert and Mary had stopped eating. "What'd he say?" Tolbert asked.

"He's mad all right," Calvin said. "But it's a quiet mad."

"That's the worst kind," Tolbert said.

"He didn't hold forth about it," Calvin went on. "Als't he said was that our good name was ruined."

Ruined. I thought of things ruined. A corncob doll I'd left out in a flooding rain. Or a hog if a wildcat got hold of it. But a name? Our name was still McCoy, wasn't it? How could it be ruined?

"He said old Devil Anse did this to him on purpose. That it was the onliest way he could strike out at him. And that we'll just have to show him, is all."

Tolbert nodded. "What's Pa want?"

"Wants you to ride over to West Virginny tomorrow and bring Ro home."

I almost knocked over my glass of milk. But all Tolbert did was nod. "Alone?"

"No," Calvin said. And then he looked at me. "Wants you to take Fanny with you, bein' as she's Ro's favorite."

I had all I could do to keep from jumping up and down and yelling yes, yes, I'll go. But I knew enough to keep a still tongue in my head.

"Alifair wants to know if you knew anything about Ro not bein' wed, Fanny?" Calvin asked. "She thinks you knew all along."

Before I had a chance to answer, Tolbert did for me. "Tell Alifair to mind her own business. And stop picking on Fanny, or she'll answer to me. She damn near drowned her today."

"I wasn't to home," Calvin said. "I was fishing. Or I would of stopped it. Well, so you'll go tomorrow then? I can tell Pa?"

"You can tell him." Tolbert stood up, and he and Calvin shook hands and they walked out the door together.

———

I was up early the next morning to have breakfast with Tolbert, made by Mary even before she was out of her long nightdress. It was still half-light in the kitchen and it felt like Christmas for the excitement. I was to go with Tolbert to bring Ro home. Just him and me! And I didn't have to go to school and answer to Mr. Cuzlin why I'd run off yesterday. Tolbert said he'd write me a note about that, because I'd told him about Nancy McCoy. And that's why, I suppose, Tolbert and Mary weren't surprised at Calvin's news.

Riding through the September woods with Tolbert was certainly a sight better than going to school. That's when I asked him about our sheep. Because that was when I still thought that sheep, and people, always came home because they knew they belonged there.

Chapter Nine

1880

TOLBERT GAVE A holler to let them know we were coming. Else they might have shot at us. At once their dogs started braying and yelping. They do have a parcel of dogs. But the family was smaller than ours. At last count, seven children, though we'd heard that Levicy Hatfield was expecting again.

Robert E. Lee, who was thirteen, came out to the gate. His hair was so yellow it was white, and it hung over his eyes. He was munching something. I saw him, though my brother made me stay back until he knew all was safe. Tolbert leaned down from his horse and said something to Robert E. Lee, who ran right into the house to get his pa, I guess.

Bushes and flowers grew wild everywhere. I kept thinking, so this is West Virginia. But it didn't look any different from Kentucky. I could see a woman on the porch behind the climbing vines. Could that be Roseanna? Then Cap Hatfield came out of the house. He was two years younger than Johnse and blind in one eye. He was a big hand for killing. He loved to kill almost as much as he loved to eat, so I got a mite scared when he walked right up to my brother. But I knew Tolbert had his gun at the ready.

Their talk drifted on the morning air. Then Tolbert waved me forward. I trembled with excitement. I was finally going to see Roseanna! But I was scared, too. I didn't trust Cap. And I didn't think Tolbert should accept an invite unless it came from old Devil Anse himself.

Then Devil Anse came out of the house, hitching up his trousers, his long black beard reaching below his neck. His head was half bald, his nose like an eagle's, and his eyes all narrow and too close together. I slid off my horse and stood behind Tolbert.

The men walked off a piece. I heard Devil Anse ask my brother what we'd come for, heard Tolbert's reply. Then they conferred in low tones. I stood like a jackass in the rain, staring over at the porch. It was Roseanna. But it seemed like she didn't see me.

"You can go on over and say howdy, Fanny," Tolbert said.

The place seemed spooked, empty. Chickens were scratching in the dirt, and except for them and the dogs settled now under the big locust tree, nothing bestirred. The weathered boards of the house made it seem stark. What windows there were gazed at us like blank eyes. Yet at the same time I felt hidden eyes on me. I opened the creaking gate and went toward the porch. "Ro?" My voice faltered.

"Fanny?"

It was Ro! I went up the rickety steps. There she was, behind the wild vines, quilting.

"Oh, my God, baby, come here." She held out her arms.

I went to her, sobbing. "Oh, Ro, I've missed you so. It's just awful at home without you."

"Why have you and Tolbert come? Is it Ma? Is she all right?"

I wiped my tears. "Yes. We've come to fetch you home. Pa sent for you."

"Pa? Pa sent for me?" She pulled back, holding me by my shoulders. "Pa? You telling me he wants me home? I thought he'd be madder than a stuck pig because of what I did."

I couldn't lie. "He is, Ro. But now he's found out you aren't wed, so he wants you home."

"Oh, Lordy, Lordy." She released me and started walking on the rickety porch, chewing on a fingernail. "How'd he find out?"

"Word's got 'round. You know how it does."

She knew. Now she folded her arms across her middle and groaned. "We wanted to marry. We still both want it. But Johnse's pa won't allow it."

I stared at her, blinking. "How can he stop you?"

"Johnse isn't twenty-one yet. But oh, honey, we love each other. And we're wed in our hearts, where it matters. No preacher could make it more legal!"

At that moment I understood more the habits of our

sheep than I understood my sister Ro. I only knew she was in trouble if she didn't come home with us today. And that was enough. "Since you're not married, you'll come home with us, won't you?" I asked.

She stopped pacing. "Oh no, Fanny, I can't come home. I can't leave Johnse. I love him."

"But you could come back when he comes of age and wed. Can't you?"

She shook her head of curly hair. "It's not only Johnse. I know Pa, Fanny. He wants me home same's he wanted that sow and pigs years ago. Because I'm his'n. But how will he treat me if I come home? You can't tell me he isn't frothing at the mouth 'cause of what I did. Can you?"

No, I couldn't.

"If I leave Johnse and go home and Pa is mean to me, I won't be able to stay. Then I'll have lost Johnse, too. He'll think I don't love him if I leave now. No, baby, I can't chance it."

Tolbert came on the porch and hugged her. "Why aren't you wed, Ro?" he asked.

"Johnse's pa won't let us."

Gently, he led her to the far end of the porch and spoke softly to her for a while, his head bent low above hers. Then I heard him finish. "You oughtn't to stay someplace with somebody if they won't let you wed, Ro," he said.

"I know." She put her hand on his arm and smiled up at him. "But Tolbert, we're working on old Devil Anse. I'm sure he'll give in soon. Did you ever know anybody who couldn't give in to me, Tolbert?"

He shrugged.

"Go on now," she said. "It isn't that I'm not glad to see you, but don't stay around too long. There could be trouble. Give my love to Ma and everybody. I'll be fine."

Tolbert didn't know what to do. He looked in the direction of old Devil Anse Hatfield and Cap, who were standing away a little piece, all the time watching us. He looked at Ro. I could tell he was split down the middle just like that old locust tree in our yard that was struck by lightning last summer. "Hate to leave you here like this," he said.

"Go. Please." She stood on tiptoe and kissed him. "I'm just fine."

Tolbert moved away, off the porch toward the gate. "Make it quick, Fanny," he said.

Was he still counting on me to convince her to come? I searched around in my mind for something to say. Then I saw the quilt she'd been working on. It was the strangest quilt I'd ever seen. All dark colors, not bright and purty like ours. "You're working on this?" I asked.

"Yes. Johnse's ma had started it and never finished. It's a Coffin quilt."

I looked closely. All around the edges were coffins, spaced well apart. The middle had a large empty space. "A Coffin quilt?"

She gave a little laugh. "I don't cotton to it much myself, but it's over half done and it's all I've got right now for our bed. Each coffin has a name of the member of the family. And when they die you move the coffin from the edge and put it in the middle. See?"

I looked up at my sister. "How can you live with

people who make quilts with coffins on them? What kind of people are they?"

"It's only a quilt, honey. Don't take on so."

"Coffins on a quilt! How can you cover yourself with it? These people are all crazy, Ro."

"It'll keep us warm this winter. When it's done I'll start on my own. Maybe one with birds, animals, and flowers."

"Ro, come home. Bad things will happen to you here, I know it."

She kissed my forehead. "Go," she said. "If you can get away, bring me a bundle of my things. Pa hasn't thrown them away, has he?"

"No." I wished I'd thought to bring her something. I thought, guiltily, of the comb. It wasn't right for a woman not to be dowered, was it? But then, Ro wasn't wed. Oh, I was so confused.

"Then maybe sometime you can ride over with them. Leave them by the gate. If I see you, I'll come out. You can do that for me, can't you? I'll warn them you may be coming, so you don't have to be afraid."

I couldn't believe she wouldn't come home with us. I bit my bottom lip to keep from crying.

Coffins on a quilt! I looked at it, lying there, ugly as sin. Then at her, so beautiful. Would she become like them if she stayed here? They were sharp-faced, ugly people, with no color in their faces. I turned and ran through the yard and the gate to where Tolbert was waiting.

Chapter Ten

1880

THE ONLIEST TIME I ever saw my pa cry was when a letter came to him, all stained and wrinkled, telling him a man he'd fought the war with had died. They'd eaten rats together in a Yankee prison. And when Pa got the letter that the man was run down by a carriage on the streets of Richmond, he cried like a baby.

That was the onliest time I saw him cry until Tolbert told him Ro wouldn't come home. Pa didn't really cry, but his face got all screwed up like he was fixing to. "Go on into the house," he said to me gruffly. "Your ma's got supper awaitin'. Tell her I'll be in directly."

By the time Tolbert brought him into the house, his face was smooth again. We all stood around the table until Pa sat. That was the custom. Then Ma would say a prayer. But soon as it was over Pa stood again, and we stopped reaching and grabbing for the food. We knew he was going to hold forth.

"Your sister has refused to come home," he said. "I say she's made her own bed, now let her lie in it. But I want to hear what you all say. First you, Sarah."

"I say we should give her another chance. Let her mull things," Ma said.

Tolbert, who'd stayed for supper, spoke next. "Her head is muddled. I think she may come if we give her time."

"I say let her sleep in the bed she made," from Alifair.

"You would say that," Pharmer flung at her. "You were always jealous of Ro. I'm for giving her another chance, Pa. Then go fetch her. We fetch our hogs when they don't come home, don't we? Can we do any less for Ro?"

"Storm the place and get her back," from Bud, "whether she wants to come or not."

"I'm with Bud," Bill said.

"Ro hasn't done anything lots of other girls haven't done," Calvin offered. "She went there thinking she was to wed. It isn't her fault the old man won't let them."

Pa took it all in, nodded after each offering. He didn't ask me or Adelaide or Trinvilla. They didn't care, but I did. And I had to say my piece. "Pa?" I asked.

"You're too young," Alifair interrupted.

"Let her speak," from Pa. "She was there. What do you have to say, Fanny?"

Everybody was looking at me, especially Alifair. She was giving me the hatefulest look I'd ever seen. "Ro's afeared you'll be mean to her if she comes home. She said she won't be able to bear it. And then she'd lose Johnse, too."

Pa nodded.

"Is she happy there?" Ma asked.

"She seems so," I said. "But we can't leave her there anyways. We have to go and ask her again to come home. I think she would if we asked her again, Pa."

"What are you telling us, Fanny child?" Ma asked.

I looked straight into my mother's careworn face. "Ma," I whispered, "she's been working on a quilt. Not like the kind we make. It has little coffins all 'round the edges, with one for everybody in the family. And when a person dies they move the coffin to the middle."

Ma closed her eyes, and I saw her lips move in prayer. Then she said the prayer aloud. "Sufficient unto the day is the evil thereof," she said. "Ranel? You hear that? You hear what kind of people they are? They've got our daughter working on a Coffin quilt."

Pa sighed heavily and gave the hand signal that we should all start to eat. "That's decided me," he said. "Tolbert, can I prevail upon you to go and see your sister again tomorrow and try to bring her home?"

"You can, Pa. But what'll convince her to come?"

"When you tell her," Pa said, "that I aim to kill every Hatfield in Kentucky and West Virginia if she doesn't come. Can I prevail on you to give her that message, Tolbert?"

"Yes, Pa," Tolbert said.

"Fanny, you're to go along with him," Pa ordered.

I felt a thrill of importance. Alifair's look grew more

hateful. "Not fair!" she whined. "Not fair she goes again. I'm the oldest. It's my place!"

"When the time comes for the fighting, Alifair, you'll be right in on it, I promise," Pa said.

So I got to go home with Tolbert again that night. And the next day we set off again for West Virginia. I asked if I could bring some of Ro's things in a bundle, but Pa said no. "She won't be needing her things if she comes home, and if she doesn't she won't be getting them. It's up to you, Fanny, to tell your sister that."

So I TOLD her. Right after Tolbert told her what Pa aimed to do if she didn't come.

"You want to start a war, Roseanna?" he asked her. I stood right next to him when he said it. "You think the last one was bad? If Pa gets all the McCoys together and storms over here, it'll be worse than the firing on Sumter."

As Ambrose Cuzlin would say when he picked up his switch, "The preliminaries are over." No more sweet words from Tolbert, no more cajoling. Ro had already told my brother again all about how much she loved Johnse, but Tolbert was not interested in hearing of it.

"Either he marries you today or Pa comes riding in here tomorrow, Ro," he said.

I held her hand. She needed me to do that. Johnse was nowhere in sight. His father, old Devil Anse, stood a distance away with two of his sons, Robert E. Lee and Elliot Rutherford. They were waiting. They knew trouble was in the air.

"I don't want anybody to get shot on my account," she said.

"Then you know what to do," Tolbert said.

She looked down at me. She patted my head. "Did you bring my things, baby?"

"Pa wouldn't let me, Ro. He said if you come home you won't be needing them, and if you don't you won't be getting them. Please come, Ro."

She nodded. Her face was white and drawn. She looked older of a sudden. "I have to talk to Johnse first," she said. And she disappeared around the corner of the house.

Tolbert and I waited on the porch. I saw Cap wandering around by the barn. He had a seven-shot repeating carbine in his hands. I nudged Tolbert.

"I know, Fanny. I saw him. Don't look at him is all."

"Will he stop us from taking Ro?"

"I'd like to see him try."

In about ten minutes my sister came back, wiping her eyes with her hand. In the other hand she had a bundle of things. The bundle was wrapped with the Coffin quilt. "I'm ready," she sniffed.

"You can ride double with Fanny," Tolbert told her.

"But one of these days me and Johnse will be wed properlike. Then nobody can keep us apart."

"When that day comes I won't stop you," Tolbert told her. "It's just that you gotta abide by notions of respectability and not sully our name."

"You're not bringing that quilt, Ro," I said.

"I aim to finish it before we wed."

"Can't you start another one?"

Tolbert scowled at her, then said to me, "Leave her be. And let's get out of here."

He helped Ro up behind me on the horse. He tied her things in the ugly Coffin quilt to the side of the saddle. As we started out of the Hatfield place, I felt dozens of eyes on our backs. I held my breath, waiting for the crack of Cap Hatfield's rifle. I thought, *No good will come of this. Some things just bode evil.* I wished she hadn't brought that Coffin quilt. *No good will come of it,* I thought, *no good at all.*

Chapter Eleven

1880

"YOU'RE NOT A-BRINGIN' that quilt into this house." Those were the first words Pa said to Ro when we got back.

"It's all I got from Johnse," she told him. "I come home like you wanted. I was doing middling well there. But I'm here now, and I aim to finish my quilt."

I held my breath while she faced Pa down. We all did, because everybody had gathered round to see her. The facing down went on for a full minute before Pa spoke again.

"You look like the hind wheels of bad luck," he said. "Bring your quilt in if you set such store by it. But don't let me see one name of this family on those coffins, you hear? Nary a McCoy name goes on it, not even yourn."

"I hear," Ro said. So the Coffin quilt came into our house.

Those were the last words Pa said to her for the next month.

———

RO SETTLED IN, but it wasn't the same. Sometimes in the night I heard her tossing and turning on her bed and whispering Johnse's name. One moon-flooded night when I knew she was awake, I went over to kneel by her bed. "Ro," I said, "what is it like to love a body like you love Johnse?"

She thought for a spell. Then she answered. "It's like being at the door of hell sometimes," she said. "And other times it's like being at the door of heaven itself."

I vowed then that I would never love anybody like that. Look what it had done to Ro. She didn't eat right anymore. Her face was thin, her eyes had dark circles under them. And sometimes in the middle of the day I'd catch her on the edge of the woods, retching. She worked on the Coffin quilt, though. Said the quicker she finished it, the quicker she'd hear from Johnse. It came to be like an amulet to her, I think.

"Don't tell Mama," she'd say, when I caught her retching in the woods.

"Why? She'll make you some black snakeroot tea."

"It won't fix what I've got," she said.

She was sick. Likely she had stomach worms from living at the Hatfields'. How long could she keep that from Mama?

Somehow she did. While I was in school that October she helped Ma dry the fruits and berries. She picked the little wild crab apples and pawpaws. She helped Ma cure meat and store the sweet potatoes. And she took Alifair's snide looks and hurtful remarks without sassing her back.

"I hope you're happy," Alifair said to her one day in the kitchen. "The bad feeling in this house is as thick as molasses."

"It's nothing like the feeling in my heart," Ro answered.

"I've never seen Pa so cast down," Alifair went on. "Can't you see how cast down he is?"

"I see nothing else, sister," Ro said. "He hasn't spoken a word to me since I came home."

"Well then?" Alifair asked. "Why don't you do something about it?"

"Onliest thing I can do is leave," Ro said.

To that Alifair said nothing, but that nothing was as powerful as the preacher on Sunday when he described hellfire to us. It was only the two of them in the kitchen. They didn't know I was listening right outside the door.

On the fifteenth, and I remember it was the fifteenth because lots of kids weren't in school but home for foddering time, Mr. Cuzlin let us out early.

That's when I saw Yeller Thing again.

I was walking home a little ways back from Adelaide and Trinvilla. The morning had been all blue and gold and the leaves on the trees were the colors of honey and blood. But by afternoon a wind had picked up, dark clouds scudded across the sky, and the sun disappeared. Right after we passed the holler where Belle Beaver lived, I felt a sense of doom. And of a sudden the chattering birds and critters got all quiet.

It was by the wood bridge that crossed Cattail Creek that I saw it.

Something went flashing by in the corner of my eye. I stopped and looked, but there was nothing there. Nothing to see, that is, but I knew something was about and lurking. I shivered. The day had turned cold. I felt disquieted, like the wind boded bad things.

Again I heard the whoosh of something streaking by. And then I smelled it, worse than a skunk by daylight. Worse than six outhouses in July.

Next I heard the growl, low and menacing one minute, high and screeching the next. It echoed in the woods. It bounced off the water in the creek. It was Yeller Thing all right. I stopped dead in my tracks. Maybe if I didn't move, he would leave me be. Oh why hadn't I made a cross in the dirt with my toe, spit in it, and made a wish when I left the house this day? I'd become careless is why. Ro was home. I thought there would be no more danger.

I can't say how many times Yeller Thing streaked by me, but I could feel the tremors he made. It was like the very earth shook each time he passed. And he seemed to be getting closer and closer with each passing.

Nothing to do but run, I decided. So I ran, fast as I could, right over that creek bridge, down the path in the woods where Adelaide and Trinvilla were walking, right past them and on up the hill. I knew he wouldn't bother them. It was me he was after. I ran so hard I never looked around, but I could still feel Yeller Thing whooshing around me. One time I even felt his hot breath. It smelled like hog-killing day.

I fell once, right on my knee. Skinned it till it bled, but I got right up and kept on, all the time sobbing. Because I was scared, yes. But more because I knew that something awful was a-goin' to happen and Yeller Thing had come to tell me. What would it be?

———

IT WAS LATER on that night in our room, when she was working on her Coffin quilt, that Ro told me she was going to have a baby.

I stared at her, not understanding at first. Oh, I knew about babies, and how they came to be. I reckon I didn't want to understand. And she laughed a little while she stitched away on that old Coffin quilt. She had the names of everybody in the Hatfield family on each little coffin along the edges by now. Her stitching was so neat, better than Ma's even.

"Well," she said, and she gave me that heartbreaking smile of hers. "A wood's colt is what it'll be, Fanny. That's what they call babies when the parents aren't married. Isn't it?"

"What will Ma and Pa say?" I asked.

"I haven't told them yet, Fanny. Haven't told anybody but you. And you mustn't tell, either. Not until I find someplace to go and stay."

I said nothing. I hugged my pillow in front of me. She was leaving again. I might have known this wouldn't last. Of course it wasn't right, her being home, and her and Pa steppıng around each other like they were step-ping around coachwhip snakes.

"Where will you go, Ro?"

"Well, I've been studying on it. And I think I'll ask Aunt Betty if I can stay with her for a while."

I nodded. Aunt Betty lived in Stringtown. She was wed to Ma's brother Allen McCoy. She had eleven young 'uns, but only three were left at home.

"It's not far," Ro said. "You can come and see me whenever you want."

"What will happen when you have the baby, Ro? Will Johnse and you wed then?"

"Oh, I'm sure, honey. Why, soon's he finds out about it, I'm sure we'll wed. And once we present his folks and ours with a new grandchild everything will be fine again. You'll see."

I wished she wouldn't use that tone. It was the same tone she used when she'd tell me stories and they came out all right in the end. I went back to bed, staring into the dark so hard I soon felt part of it. This wasn't going to come out all right in the end, no matter how Ro tried to wash it over. I'd seen Yeller Thing, hadn't I? That's why he'd come to me today. To warn me. To let me know things weren't going to come out right. Ever.

Chapter Twelve

1880

RO WENT TO Stringtown to talk to Aunt Betty. She brought gifts, a jar of fruit vinegar, and some crab-apple jelly. You don't visit hereabouts without bringing something from your larder.

"Do you want me to get word to Johnse about the baby?" I asked. It was early of a morning, the whispery part where even the birds speak in hushed voices.

"No time," she said.

"I'll make time. He should know, Ro. Isn't right his not knowing." Was she going to keep it from him, then?

"He and his family are off timbering," she said.

It was the old of the moon. A good time for timbering. A good time for cutting hay, too, which was where Pa and my brothers had gone at first light. They never cut on the new of the moon, because the sap was still in the hay and it'd take longer to dry.

My family planted and harvested by the signs. The

rules for this are simple. You plant in the fruitful signs of Scorpio, Pisces, Taurus, or Cancer. You plow in Aries. You plant flowers in Libra when the moon is in the first quarter. It goes on like that and you dasn't go against the rules or corn will have small ears, potatoes will get nubs, and if you kill a hog in the growing parts of the moon the meat gets all puffy. Lots of town people just hoot about this, but it works for us so we keep doing it.

I had to go to school, so I couldn't go to Aunt Betty's with Ro. All day I thought about her. About that little bitty baby growing inside of her and her having to find someplace to stay because Pa would go crazy if he found out about it. She knew that as well as I did. All that jabber about the baby bringing people together was so much sassafras.

I half wished Aunt Betty would say no, that Ro couldn't live with her. She still had three young 'uns at home and it'd be a bad example for them having Ro around, her not being wed and all. Wouldn't it? But I knew the answer to that one, too.

Aunt Betty was the kindest creature around these parts who ever drew breath. She was a true Christian, good to everybody. She never talked about sin or hellfire. She just went about in her sweet way, and her door was open to anyone who was in need. So I wasn't surprised when Ro came home in two days laden with blackberry jelly, huckleberry puffs, fig pudding, and the news that she was moving in with Aunt Betty.

She told that at supper. Pa said nothing, because he never spoke to her. Ma just blinked. "Leaving us again, Ro? Now why?"

I waited for my sister to tell them about the baby. In the next moment, silent except for the clinking of forks, I saw Alifair watching her. Just like a fox. And it came to me. Alifair suspected about the baby. Oh, how she'd love to know. She couldn't wait for Ro to do something more to fall farther from grace. She'd be the first one to hop up from the table and move Ro's pebble on Ma's rock to the side of the damned, after it had been moved back to the side of the saved, too.

"I just feel like a burden here," Ro said.

"Kin are never a burden," Ma reminded her.

"I know," Ro said softly, "but things are disquieted since I'm home, and I have no right to disquiet this family."

Everyone waited for Pa to say something then. But my sister might as well have been speaking in tongues for all the mind Pa paid to her. He wasn't about to break his silence nohow. So Ro packed her things and left the next day for Aunt Betty's in Stringtown. She took the Coffin quilt with her.

"You're the only one who knows about the baby," she told me before she left. "I expect you to keep my secret, long as it can be kept."

I'd die first before I told. I'd let myself be hauled into the woods by Yeller Thing. Didn't she know that?

Things quieted down somewhat after she took her leave. But I missed her sore bad. *Does Ma suspect the real reason?* I wondered. You had to get up awful early in the morning to fool her.

I decided to test her. "I'm so sad Ro had to leave us,"

I said one day while helping out in the kitchen. "Aren't you, Ma?"

We were alone. I'd never say such if Alifair was around. When I was alone with Ma she sometimes said things she wouldn't say around the others. Now she said something I wish I hadn't been privy to.

"You know what we believe, Fanny," she said. "That God predestines all things, good and bad. That the bad is for God's purpose. That it serves some good. All evil brings out the good in people."

I reckon it was right about then that I stopped being a Primitive Baptist, if I ever was one. I didn't see what good could come out of Pa's not talking to my sister, of Ro's having a baby and the father not knowing it, of her having to live with Aunt Betty because she knew her family wouldn't have her under their roof if they knew of it.

I never spoke to Ma about it again. We did our chores, went to school, to church. The colors in the woods deepened. The nights grew cold. Frost covered everything in the mornings. In church one Sunday the preacher said the end was at hand. "We're in the last evening of time," he said. "As far as when the end comes, Scripture tells us 'even the angels in heaven won't know.' But I do believe we're in the evening of time, and we'd all best prepare for it."

They don't fool around in our church. They get right to things. But at least we're not as bad as the people who handle snakes to prove that God is looking out for them. I like to think that we don't need to handle snakes to prove God loves us. Or stand around getting the jimjams about being consumed in fire. I like to think about God as somebody kind and loving. Somebody who'd like my sister Ro's baby right off. Maybe give it dimples, even though she wasn't married to Johnse Hatfield when she was having it.

Anyways, things seemed to settle down after Ro left. Or so I thought. But I soon found different. I soon found that once evil gets into your house, it slithers around there like a cold mist. Sometimes even hides in the corners. But it's there once you let it in and you can't get shut of it.

How did it get in? With that Coffin quilt of Ro's. That quilt smelled of evil. And I think Mrs. Hatfield gave it to Ro so the evil could touch her. And us.

Anyways, evil doesn't lie still too long. Any more than a Hoop snake. After a week or two things started happening. Real fast, too.

It started the day I rode over to Aunt Betty's to see Ro. That was the day I found out she'd put her own name on one of the little coffins on the edge of the Coffin quilt. And if that wasn't enough, it was the day Johnse came to visit.

Chapter Thirteen

FALL 1880

"I'm scared, Floyd," I said.

My brother looked up from his carving. He was making a baby cradle. Wood shavings were all around his feet. On the shelf in front of a big window sat little horses, bows and arrows, some corn guns, and a wooden dancing bear. The place smelled of wood and wood shavings. I watched his strong hands caress the wood, testing it for smoothness. He often made cradles for people. Was this one for Ro? Did he know about her baby? Might be he did. She came to talk to him, too, here in his little cabin when the notion took her. But if it was for Ro, he'd never say. And I wouldn't ask.

"I heard a mourning dove last night," I told him. "Ma says they only call when there's somebody to mourn. I'm a-goin' to see Ro today. And I'm scared of what I'll find."

He eyed me from beneath long lashes. Women went

crazy over Floyd when he went to dances and such. "Seen any turtle doves of late?" he asked.

"Saw one this morning."

"Know what that means, don't you? That somebody loves you and sent the turtle dove to tell you. Likely he was bringing a message to Ro from Johnse."

"Why'd he come here? And not go to Aunt Betty's?"

"Likely nobody told him she wasn't here anymore." Floyd wasn't spoiling for a fight with the Hatfields, like most other McCoys. He liked to live peaceable with everybody. Besides, both McCoys and Hatfields bought his toys.

"Bill's pebble is on the damned side of Ma's rock," I said. I could talk to Floyd about such things, being as he held himself a bit away from the family. He loved them and would never let me bad-mouth them, but he wouldn't let them hold sway over him, either.

"That's 'cause he went hunting last Sunday and never came for Meeting."

"Do you think he's damned?"

"No."

"Do you think the Devil is wagering for Ro's soul, like Pa says?"

"No more than he's wagering for everybody else's."

I felt everything inside me settling. "After today, it's likely my pebble will be with Bill's."

He raised one eyebrow. "They don't know you're going to see her?"

"No. Which is why I couldn't bring her anything from the house. I wish I had something to bring her."

He reached around and fumbled behind him for a

moment. He took something from a shelf and handed it to me. It was small, round, and smooth.

"A stone," I said.

"Not just a stone. A madstone. Taken from the stomach of a deer. It can draw poison from a snakebite."

The stone lay warm in my hand. I rubbed my fingers over it. "Thank you, Floyd."

"I'll be sending her something else soon," he said.

I nodded. "You won't be telling where I went today if they ask?"

"'Course not. Go on with you. And be careful in the woods."

———

VERDY, VIOLA, AND Maelene, Aunt Betty's three girls, weren't home, thank heaven. I'd never liked them. They were a bit younger than Ro, not married yet, and smitten with men. All they did was fuss over themselves and make new dresses. I know they didn't like Ro because she was purtier than all three of them put together.

Aunt Betty hugged me and gave me a glass of buttermilk and some fresh cookies to take outside where Ro was sitting under the mimosa tree, sewing. "Glad somebody's come to see her," she whispered. "She's pining away for home." I could tell she was worried about Ro because Aunt Betty baked when she worried. Now wisps of gray-white hair framed her round pleasant face. The kitchen was hot and full of cakes and pies. She must have been baking all morning.

"Is she still working on that Coffin quilt, Aunt Betty?"

"She's right now sewing a coffin on the edge for her baby," she said. "I know that some people in these parts use such quilts as family records. But it's downright tempting fate to put a baby coffin on one. Go on and talk to her. Your sunny little face will do her good, honey."

I knew my face wasn't sunny. Neither was I. But I went out to find Ro, setting the milk and cookies down on a wooden bench. "How you feeling, Ro?"

She stopped stitching and looked past me, dreamily. "Do you know that there's a little creek down there name of Devil's Jump? It's all full of boulders and rocks and such. They say the Devil passed by here with his apron full of rocks. He proposed to burden the land with them, but his apron string busted and he dropped the rocks right there in the creek."

It wasn't like Ro to set store in tales about the Devil like most people in these mountains did. She was brooding. "How you coming with the quilt?" I asked.

"It'll be done soon."

"That's a mighty little coffin there. Who's it for?"

She smiled. "My baby."

"Afore it's born? You know Pa said he didn't want any McCoy names on the quilt."

"He's not here, is he? Anyways, it's not *for* the baby. When it comes, I'll put its name there and date of birth. It's a record of sorts. See here? Here's a little coffin for the little 'un Johnse's mother is expecting."

A chill went through me. "Got a present for you from Floyd." I gave her the madstone.

She took it up, smiled, and held it in her hand. "It's

still warm from his touch. It holds the warmth of the person who takes it from the stomach of the deer, you know. That's right nice of Floyd. Thank him for me. How's things to home?"

I shrugged. "The same."

"They know you're here today?"

"No. But you know I'm always allowed to wander free on Saturday as I please."

"I'd rather you visit me than anybody," she said. "And since you've come, there's a promise I want from you, Fanny."

I felt a sense of doom, like the sun just left the heavens. "What?"

"I know you don't like this quilt, but that's just because you don't understand it. Promise me that if anything ever happens to me or my baby, you'll move our coffins to the center and make sure my baby's name and date of birth and death get put on right."

I stared at my beautiful sister. I'd heard people talk of how women who were expecting a baby got all kinds of strange notions and had to be humored. Was this one of them? Or was Ro suddenly getting strange in the head?

"Why should anything happen to you or your baby?" I asked.

"Just promise me you'll do as I ask, Fanny. And then keep the quilt forever."

A chilly breeze stirred the branches of the mimosa tree. From the kitchen came Aunt Betty's singing. "Queen Jane" was the song. I knew of it. Calvin explained how it told how Henry the Eighth, who had his wives' heads cut off, followed Jane Seymour, one of them, to the grave. And how lots of our songs are handed down from the Old World, from England. He said that's why we say things like "afeared." Because Shakespeare did, too.

Ro was waiting for me to answer. But I recollected what Tolbert had told me once, "Don't ever be pushed into a promise. Say you'll study on it."

"I'll study on it," I told her.

Did she hear me? Of a sudden someone whistled, clear and sharp on the fall air, from the direction of Devil's Jump. Ro stood. The quilt tumbled from her lap. "Oh, it's Johnse! I knew he'd come. I knew he couldn't stay away."

I watched her fly across the grass down to the creek. I sat there munching Aunt Betty's sugar cookies. The Coffin quilt had landed on my lap.

Chapter Fourteen

FALL 1880

I SPIED ON them. Those are the only words to put on what I did that day when Ro met Johnse Hatfield near Devil's Jump. I hid behind some rocks that the Devil had dropped conveniently when his apron string busted and listened to what they said to each other.

After they finished hugging and kissing that is. And they did that for some time. I thought they'd never stop, but finally they did and that's when I listened.

He told her how he'd heard she was here. He asked her why.

She told him it was because she just couldn't live under Pa's roof, with his hate creeping around her like a ginseng vine around a tree. "And I haven't even told you about the baby yet."

That's when Johnse broke loose from her and looked like he'd just been hit by one of the boulders dropped from the Devil's apron. "Baby?" he asked.

You can picture what followed. Lots more hugging and kissing, which was only proper, I reckon. Ro got all shy then, like she never got with anybody. And I wondered if the Devil was indeed wagering for her soul.

"Can we go into the house and talk?" he asked.

"No," she said. "Wouldn't be fair to Aunt Betty if she let you in, being as we're not wed. She's courting gossip just letting me stay with her."

"All right," he said. "We'll talk here. It isn't that I'm not happy about the baby, Ro. How couldn't I be? But we've got to do something. I don't want my child a wood's colt."

"What'll we do?" she asked.

They studied on the matter. Like there was all kinds of things for them to do when both knew there was only one. Get hitched. And both knew how impossible it was.

"Do you think we could?" she asked.

Johnse shook his head. "Onliest way is if we ran off. Got shut of this place and everybody around here."

"Then how would we live?" Ro asked. "There'd be nobody to help us raise a house or give us a start. You know how important that is, Johnse. And neither one of us has got a penny to our name."

They brooded some more. "We'll figure a way," he said. "And next time I come, I'll have an answer. I promise you, darlin'. I'll be back next week. Meet me here by this creek. One week from today."

I got out from behind that old boulder then and crept away, back to the mimosa tree, all the while trying to figure out how to help them. It wasn't right they couldn't wed. I knew that, young as I was. Just the same as I knew that you wash your head with apple vinegar if you get cooties.

Ro didn't talk much for the rest of our visit. Just went back to work on that old Coffin quilt of hers like nothing had happened. She sure was set on stitching that baby's little black coffin down firm.

Aunt Betty asked me to stay for supper, but I said no, I had to get home. I could stay away "in the woods" just so long, even on a Saturday, without having to explain where I was.

"Can I come back next Saturday?" I asked Ro. I didn't want her to run off with Johnse without me knowing it.

She said yes. And made no connection to Johnse's coming again. It was like she was someplace else in her head and didn't even know I was leaving.

———

I MUST HAVE been someplace else in my head, too, not to reckon that Johnse could pay a visit to my sister without word getting around like a brush fire. By the time I came to the supper table my whole family knew he'd been there.

My brothers Bill and Bud brought the news. They'd been to Stringtown that morning, to the general store run by old Harlan Meeker, to get some coffee beans for Ma. I loved my brothers, but I didn't believe the story. Why to Stringtown, when we had a right proper general store here and Mr. Randolph sometimes gave us goods on trade?

No. I didn't believe a word of how they'd just happened to run into Johnse and stood jawing with him a while, real friendly-like. I think my brothers were snooping around like bloodhounds. My family can be awful sneaky sometimes.

"What's Johnse doing in Stringtown?" Pa asked.

"Maybe buying coffee beans," Alifair said. She got right uppity sometimes, and Pa let her 'cause she was the oldest girl and he said she had common sense and depended on her.

"He was to see Ro," Pa said. "And by Jehoshaphat, I won't abide it!" He slapped his hand on the table and we all got quiet. I'd been quiet all along, of course, scared somebody would know I'd been to see her this day.

"Not gonna have it," Pa was ranting. "He's seen the last of my daughter, that little white maggot."

I felt Alifair staring at me, like she knew I'd seen Ro that afternoon. Her eyes looked downright queer, like she was looking right into my soul. And I began to believe that she did have powers, like Ma said. I kept my eyes down on my plate, because I didn't want to face her power just then, whatever it was.

"Tell you what I want, boys," Pa said to Bud and Bill. "Want you both to go to Stringtown next Saturday and keep an eye on that little white maggot. He'll be timbering with his pa all week, but sure's God made apples, he'll be on the prowl again next Saturday. If you sense he's on his way to see Ro, come tell me. I'll get Jim to arrest him. He's deputy sheriff. It's his job to arrest people who seduce innocent young girls."

It was the first time since Ro had run off with Johnse that he'd spoken of her as innocent. Would my brother Jim really arrest Johnse? Could he arrest him? What did *seduce* mean? Had Johnse done something terrible to Ro that I didn't know about? If so, why had they clung together at Devil's Jump today like the Devil was coming back again with his apron full of stones?

Alifair was staring at me again. I quickly looked down. She could wither my spirit, that girl, if she tried hard enough.

"Don't you think somebody ought to go over and warn Ro that Johnse is sneaking around?" Ma asked. "I'm sure she doesn't want to see him anymore. If she did, why would she be hiding out at Aunt Betty's?"

Young as I was, sometimes I thought that my ma had too much religion, that it had addled her brain.

Pa stopped shoving food in his mouth long enough to stare at her. "You telling me, Sarah, that our daughter doesn't want to see him anymore?"

"She was mighty put out with him for not going against old Devil Anse and marrying her, Ranel. I know that much. I think she should be warned. Haven't we had enough tribulation in this family?"

Pa nodded and allowed that we had. *If they knew about the baby they'd know about tribulation,* I thought. They'd be out hunting Johnse right now with repeater rifles. Nobody knew, except me and maybe Floyd. And we weren't telling.

Of a sudden I lost my taste for the food, worrying for Ro. Suppose next Saturday my brother Jim did arrest

Johnse? I had to warn Ro somehow. I started planning how while my family fussed all around me. I prayed, sitting there. *Dear Lord, show me the way.* And then for some reason, maybe it was blind luck like happens to you sometimes, God answered my prayer.

Pa decided Ro should be warned. And that I was the one to do it.

"I'll have to take a day off from school," I said.

"No," Pa decreed. "It can wait. Johnse won't be on the prowl till Saturday."

Alifair objected, of course. But this time Pa hushed her up. I was Ro's favorite, he reminded her. Onliest ones she trusted right now were me and Ma, and he wasn't about to send Ma on a child's errand. And so that's how I got to be on the scene when my brother Jim came to arrest Johnse Hatfield and we acquired more tribulation in our family. Or as my brother Tolbert would say, all hell broke loose.

Chapter Fifteen

FALL 1880

SOMETIMES PA WILL talk about the war. He'll tell how muddled he felt when he found out that Virginia, which he thought was for the Confederacy, went off and split itself in two and he was fighting for West Virginia and something different than he thought.

That's how I felt all week. Always I thought my family was all of a piece. Now Ro had broken herself off. And was on the side of something different. And me with her. I was so addle-headed I got in trouble in school. We were learning to cipher, but no matter how I studied my *Pike's Arithmetic*, I couldn't work those numbers on my slate.

"Fanny McCoy, if you take five apples away from twelve and give them to your sister, how many would you have left?" Mr. Cuzlin asked.

Dazed, I asked stupidly, "Which sister?"

Everybody laughed. Adelaide and Trinvilla were smirking at me.

Mr. Cuzlin scowled. "Which sister would you like to give five apples to, Fanny?"

"Roseanna," Nancy McCoy burst out. "She needs 'em."

More laughter. Mr. Cuzlin slammed his hand down on the desk. "The answer! Now!" Instead I glared at Nancy. "I'd give Ro all twelve if I could! But nary a one to Adelaide or Trinvilla. Or Alifair!" They watched me all the time, inside the house and out, and I knew they were reporting to Alifair. Because she still suspected I'd sneaked off to see Ro.

Mr. Cuzlin stood. "The preliminaries," he said, "are over."

I'd never gotten the switch at school and I braced myself as he came toward me. Instead he grabbed my arm and dragged me over to the side of the room with the little kids, the five-year-olds, and shoved me down in a desk. "Maybe you can learn something from them," he said.

Everybody laughed and my face went hot. I'd rather be switched. Trinvilla and Adelaide were still smirking.

———

SATURDAY FINALLY CAME and I went to see Ro again, this time with Pa's blessing. "Listen to everything she says and report to me," he said.

Again when she went to Devil's Jump to meet Johnse I followed and hid behind the boulder. I didn't want them to run off without my knowing.

94

I heard Johnse say how he told his pa about the baby. "He said he doesn't want any spawn of the McCoys under his roof." Ro gave a cry, but he gentled her and commenced telling her of his plan. To this day I believe he had a plan, and if my brother Jim and Pa hadn't rode up right then I would have heard tell of it.

But they did ride up, on horses that were lathered and wild in the eye, Jim with his gun drawn and Pa waving his hat in the air and shouting and looking like he was fulfilling some prophecy from Isaiah. They tore through the bushes on the other side of Devil's Jump, splashed their horses right into the creek, and reined them up so hard their horses reared on their hind legs.

Ro screamed as my brother Jim yelled, "Johnse Hatfield, I'm here to arrest you under the laws of the great state of Kentucky for seducing a young woman. Hand over your pistol."

Then Ro recovered herself. "Still letting Pa lead you around by the nose, I see."

Jim stood his ground. Which was now the water in the creek.

Johnse had his hands out, palms turned up. "I'd never do a thing to hurt Ro. Ask her."

Jim wasn't about to ask anybody anything right then. He aimed to carry out the proper order of things. "Come on, Johnse, let's go peaceful-like," he said. "We'll let the court decide."

"No court in Kentucky gonna give a Hatfield a fair shot," Johnse said.

"Why should they?" Ro screamed. "My own family won't give him a fair shot. Pa, how can you do this to me? Haven't you hurt me enough? When will all this stupid hatred end?"

Pa didn't even answer.

"Pa, there's no cause to do this, please!" Ro was pleading now. "I went with Johnse of my own will. He never seduced me. I love him, Pa! Why are you taking on like this?" And she sloshed through the water with her long skirts, right toward Pa and Jim.

"Don't come any farther, Ro," Jim advised.

"Why? You gonna shoot me, too? You big sheriff's deputy hero?"

"Bring him in, Jim," Pa said.

"Soon's Ro gets outa the way."

But Ro stood right in the way between Johnse and Jim, while Jim still aimed his gun at Johnse, which meant, of course, it was pointed first at Ro, and Pa kept fussing at him to get on with it. Talk about tribulation! You'd have to go all the way back to Job in the Bible to match this.

My sister started sobbing then. It was terrible sounding. "Pa," she was blubbering, "Pa, how can you do this to me?"

And Pa was saying, "I'll do more to you in a minute if'n you don't move. I'll get off this horse and you'll find out what I can do if I set my mind to it."

Right about then I figured somebody had to end it, or they'd all be standing there until the sheep came home for salt. So I ran out from behind that boulder right toward my brother. "Let him go! They love each other!"

Later on, I received a long lecture from Jim, who told me how he could have taken that movement for anything and fired his gun. And maybe killed me. Or Ro, or even Johnse. "You should have stayed out of it," he scolded. "What in tarnation were you doing there, any-ways? You didn't belong there. You're always where you don't belong, Fanny. Damn women always are!"

I didn't know whether to cry for the scolding or to be proud because he'd lumped me in with all woman-kind. But back to that creek.

Jim didn't fire. He was his old steely self, though the gun did waver a bit. One good thing, though, I'd pushed Ro out of the way.

Johnse never moved. Just stood there with his palms out. "You okay, Ro?" he asked.

"I'm fine!" She was mad now. "Fanny, get out of the way," she said. "Go on up to the house with Aunt Betty."

But I wouldn't move.

There's no telling what would have happened next if Aunt Betty hadn't come out of the house and stood there shielding her eyes with her hand and hollering, "Hello! What's going on down there? You all right, girls?"

Jim took off his hat and waved it. "Everything's fine, Aunt Betty. They'll be up in a minute!"

Aunt Betty sort of broke the mood. Everybody looked pretty shamefaced for a minute. Johnse ended it. "I'll come along, Jim. Peaceful-like. It's the only way to get this thing settled."

"No!" Ro yelled. "They'll kill you!"

"Nobody's killing anybody," Jim said quietly. "You know me better than that, Ro."

"Well, I don't know Pa. Not anymore!"

But when Jim took Johnse in hand, she hushed. She touched Johnse's arm, then stood with her hands over her mouth as Jim helped Johnse onto his horse and they started down the path, Jim leading Johnse's horse by the reins. Ro ran after them. "God, don't take him, please!" she sobbed.

"Fanny, take care of your sister," Jim ordered. Then they rode away in the name of the great state of Kentucky.

"Oh my God, oh my God, they're going to kill him!" She was bent over, sobbing.

"Come on, Ro," I said. "Don't cry."

She stopped crying then. She had another thought. "I've got to warn Anse!" she said. "If I can warn Anse Hatfield, he'll stop them! She stood up, wiped her face, looked around, and spied Aunt Betty's horse, Clothilda, in the field. "It's ten miles to the Hatfields' cabin. I can make it."

"You can't ride like you are," I said. "You'll hurt the baby." I knew that much. "And we both have wet shoes and skirts. We'll take our death of colds."

She bent over, grabbed her petticoat, and started ripping. "Help me make a halter. You can ride behind me if you want."

You take sides with somebody and there's no going back. One little bit at a time you keep opening doors and going through them, until you've got so many doors behind you, you can't find your way back nohow. In ten minutes we had the petticoat halter on the horse and were off to cross the Tug and warn the Hatfields.

Chapter Sixteen

FALL 1880

IT WAS ON that ride that I knew Ma was right all along. The Devil was wagering for Roseanna's soul. And he was winning.

What made me know this was Clothilda. She was old. Aunt Betty's children had grown up riding her. These days Aunt Betty rode her into Stringtown, at a slow and easy gait, and that was all the exercise she got. Otherwise she just lounged around in the pasture, limping.

On that ride, Clothilda was like a demon. She never held back through the ravines. She was sure-footed over rocks and fallen trees. She plowed through thickets of briars, she never got afeared of the path ahead. It was as if she *knew* the path, though she'd never been on it before. And all the while my sister was leaning low over her, whispering in her ears.

Might be it was Ro who was the demon. Don't think

I didn't ponder that, much as I had a chance to ponder anything sitting behind Ro and holding on to her for dear life. It was a wild cold ride, through hidden secret places. Not the way Tolbert had taken me at all.

We came to the river finally, the Tug at Matewan. That old Clothilda never spooked, just splashed right in. Oh, the water felt so good on my legs even though it was cold, because they were scratched and burning from the underbrush. The Tug was low. Somebody was with us on that. Ma would say God. I say it was the Devil. And the reason I know it was him was because his henchman was along with us on the ride, too.

Yeller Thing. I saw him and I smelled him as Clothilda dashed through that water, splashing white foam up all around us. I saw him through the foam. He was in the water, too, keeping up with us, growling and egging Clothilda on. I screamed. "Ro! Look!"

But she didn't look, and like as not, if she had she wouldn't have seen. Only I saw Yeller Thing, ever. Only I felt the terror of him. I knew by now that he was my terror alone and nobody else's.

———

Soon enough we were up the embankment and on West Virginia soil. More riding, though this time the way was not so harsh. And then through a path in the woods to Devil Anse's place. Dogs yowled, chickens fled as Ro pulled back on the petticoat reins and slid off Clothilda's back. "Get her some water," she said, and she ran through the yard to the house.

I sat on Clothilda, holding the petticoat reins, looking around, feeling as last time that eyes were watching me. I looked around for Yeller Thing, but all I saw at first were red-and-gold leaves, purple flowers, and pumpkins and squash in the garden.

And then I saw the people in the distance. Men. Lots of them at the far end of the road that led to the barn. Men eating at makeshift tables under the trees. And women serving them. I smelled the new timbered wood at the same time and saw it piled all around. Devil Anse was adding on to his barn and those must be his kin, helping.

My sister saw them at the same time, ran from the porch, down the lane, crying, "Help me, help me!"

"Child, what is it?" Mrs. Devil Anse, or Levicy, as they called her, came down the lane, heavy with child, to embrace my sister.

I turned my head away, jumped down from Clothilda, and went about the business of drawing a bucket of water from the well for her. No sooner did I have it up on the rim of the well than Robert E. Lee came around a corner of the house. He was so pale! His face almost as white as the hair that hung over his pale eyes.

"Howdy," he said.

I nodded and brought the water to Clothilda. I stood there while she drank it.

"Y'all got trouble?"

I shrugged. "My brother arrested yours."

"What for?"

"Seduction." I stared into his pale eyes. "I don't even know what that is, do you?"

He nodded slowly, understanding, but he didn't say.

"Y'all picked a good day fer a fight. My pa's got all his kin here. Guess I better fetch my gun." And he ran into the house.

A fight? What did he mean? Was that all these people ever paid mind to? Mrs. Devil Anse was coming toward me, her arm around Roseanna. She was clucking and hovering over Ro like she was her mother. She saw me then and held out her hand. "Child, child, come on into the house and I'll give you some warm milk and ginger-bread and put some salve on those legs," she said. And just then Robert E. Lee came bounding out of the house, gun in hand.

"I'd as lief stay out here," I said.

"Fanny, you come along now. Don't be rude. Come on, I say!" Ro never ordered me around, and she really wasn't now. But she held out her hand to me and I couldn't refuse her. So I followed them into the house and allowed myself to be sat down at the table in the kitchen and drink warm milk and eat gingerbread without shame that it was Devil Anse's milk and gingerbread. I watched Mrs. Devil Anse put salve on Ro's scratches and a cold rag to her head, and heard my sister pour out her heart about the matter to this woman about whom I'd been told since I was a knee baby had horns on top of her head.

She didn't, of course. She was as nice as my ma, if not nicer. At least she didn't rant and rave about tribulation or the vengeance of the Lord. Or run outside to put a pebble by the name of Johnse on the side of the damned on a praying rock. She comforted Ro best as she could, and when she was done made her lie down on a couch nearby. Then she attended to me.

"I told him and told him," she said to Ro as she knelt and took each of my legs at a time and applied her decoction of salve, "to let you two wed. But no. I declare these men of ourn, they have a mournful need for war. And if there's no more Blue Bellies to shoot at, why they'll just make up some!"

I decided that I liked Levicy Hatfield. She had a round, pleasant face, her kitchen smelled good, her gingerbread was the best I ever tasted, and she had common sense. I was so torn with guilt about liking her I could scarce swallow.

A minute later, when the whole parcel of men rode out, she stepped out onto the porch and yelled, "Robert E. Lee, where you think you're going?"

I heard the reply, through the tramping of horses' feet as the men left, then I saw her go off the porch through the dust and grab the reins of the pony Robert E. Lee was riding.

"Ma!" he protested. "I'm huntin' McCoys!"

But she pulled him from the pony and dragged him by the ear into the house. "Thirteen years old," she said, "and a bigger vexation to me than any of them! The only thing you're hunting is rabbits! Now get out there and cut some wood for the stove!"

I liked her even better now. And my guilt vanished.

We sat awhile until Ro was rested. Levicy took off Ro's skirt and dried it by the fire. I sat and dried mine. I was getting worried again. I'd seen as many as forty men ride off with Devil Anse to find my pa and Jim. When we got ready to leave, Ro saw my discomfort. "I won't tell Pa you were here with me," she promised.

I hugged her as we rode back to Aunt Betty's. "What if they ask?"

"Then you lie to Pa. It's the only way to survive. Haven't you learned that yet?"

I was learning. The ride back wasn't half as bad, maybe because we took our time, and maybe because all I could think of was what would happen to Pa and Jim when all those Hatfields caught up with them. I was crazy with worry about it. But then, by the time we got to Aunt Betty's, it was late. She wanted to give me supper, but I said no, I'd best get home.

"You all right, child?" she asked.

"All right as I can be in West Virginia," I said.

"What's the matter with you, Fanny?" Ro asked sharply. "You're back in Kentucky now, and you know it. If you're feverish I'll not let you go home, but stay the night."

I told them I was fine and started off. I knew I was in Kentucky all right. Did they think I was teched? But I also knew I was broken off from the family now, like West Virginia had broken from the Confederacy. I'd made my stand. And it was with my sister and against my family. I felt the break inside me already and knew it would mean trouble.

I suppose I was ready for it. A body had to be, if they made a stand. Wasn't my family always saying such? Only thing that plagued me was I still didn't know the meaning of the word *seduction*.

Chapter Seventeen

FALL 1880

I KNOW THINGS about the family and I'm the youngest. Maybe I know them *because* I'm the youngest. And they said things to me and thought I wouldn't understand. Or I stood around the edges and watched and they paid me no nevermind. And when I tell them the things I know, they say those things never happened. And so the burden of the knowing is on me.

———

"IT'S ABOUT TIME you got home! Ma's been half crazy, what with Pa and Jim riding out looking for Johnse. Did they get him? Did they come to Aunt Betty's while you were there? What are those scratches on your legs? Look at her, Ma. She's all tore up." Alifair grabbed me soon's I walked in the door. Ma and the girls stood around looking at me. But it was Adelaide with her granny-woman ways who set out to ruin me.

"Her legs have been treated with salve." Adelaide picked up my dress. "Likely dock root and sweet cream."

I pushed her away. "You leave me be!"

Alifair grabbed my arm and shook me. "Leave you be? You deserve a switching for worrying Ma so. Who treated your legs?"

I looked at Ma for sympathy, but saw none. "After Pa and Jim came and took Johnse, Ro rode off on Aunt Betty's horse after them. And when she didn't come back Aunt Betty got worried and I went looking for her. Got caught in some briars. Aunt Betty treated me."

Lie to Pa and you lie to God. Now I was lying to Ma. Was it the same? More to the point, did she believe me? I didn't care about the others. I did care about Ma.

"It was good of Aunt Betty," she said after a long moment. "But I think you ought to have a bath and soak those legs before mortification sets in. Alifair, see to it."

If Ma wanted to punish me she couldn't have picked a better way. We bathed once a week, for Sunday Meeting, but now the old tub in the cellar was filled with hot water and Alifair scrubbed me. She did not do it softly, and the more I yelled, the harder she scrubbed.

"You've been up to something," she said. "You little sneak. Ma may believe it, but I don't. I've a mind to hold your head under until you tell. Only you'll go snitch and get yourself sent to Tolbert's again, where you get spoiled rotten. But afore this is done, I'll find what you've been about and you'll be whupped good for lying. Ma can't abide lying. You know that?"

Lucky for me we heard Pa come home just then, or

might be she'd have held my head under the water. But she wanted to hear what he had to say. I dried myself, put on my nightdress, and followed her upstairs. Pa stood in the kitchen, still looking like he'd fulfilled a prophecy from Isaiah.

"We were a-takin' Johnse to the county jail at Pikeville when they rode up. Forty of 'em. Hatfields. A-gunnin' for us. Devil Anse pointed that gun of his right at me. Would of fired it, too, if Johnse didn't knock it from his hands."

"Johnse saved your life?" Ma asked.

"How did they know to seek you out?" Leave it to Alifair to hop on that like a june bug.

"Johnse only did it 'cause of Jim," Pa answered Ma. "We thought they was McCoys comin' and Jim promised, as a man of the law, to protect Johnse no matter how many McCoys."

Only Pa would put such a meaning on it.

Ma started to talk again about how Johnse saved his life, but Alifair interrupted with her big mouth. "How did the Hatfields *know*, Pa? Somebody must have told 'em."

He stopped talking and stared at her. And his face took on a look like God's must have when He caught Adam eating the apple. "Ro!" he hollered. "Why didn't I think on it? My own daughter. Yer right, Alifair, Ro told 'em. By God, my own daughter!" And he set to pacing in the kitchen like a painter cat.

"Now Ranel, ye don't know it was Ro," Ma started.

"Don't know it? Who else, I ask? Who else even knew we were there?"

Silence, terrible silence in the kitchen. Alifair turned to me with a smile on her face. "Fanny," she asked sweetly, "you were there, child. I know you're plumb wore out from today, but you did say she rode off on Aunt Betty's horse, didn't you? And you went to fetch her home and got all those scratches on your legs? You should see her legs, Pa. The poor little thing's all covered with scratches."

Now all had their eyes on me again. I felt my poor scratched legs tremble. I clenched my fists and decided that someday I'd kill my sister Alifair. How, I didn't know, but I'd think of a way.

"Fanny?" Pa asked. "When your sister rode off, did she say where she was a-goin'?"

"No, Pa. She was just so all-fired scared for Johnse. I asked her, but no, she wouldn't say."

More lying. But he believed it.

Later I lay in the darkness of my room, terrified by the awfulness of what I'd done. I couldn't sleep for fear of it. Then, when the house got quiet, the door of my room opened and Alifair stood over my bed in her long, white nightdress.

"Come with me," she said.

"Where?"

"Never you mind. You just come."

I went, following her through the darkness of the house, out into the chilly night, fearstruck. What was she going to do to me now? Her nightdress fluttered in the chill autumn breeze, like some ghostly thing ahead of me. She held a candle but didn't light it. Hooty owls called. Old Blue started fussing, but Alifair hushed him.

I followed her to Ma's tree stump, where she stopped and lit the candle. In its yellow light her face looked down at me, firm and full of purpose.

"Take your pebble and put it on the side of the damned."

I stared up at her. "That's Ma's job. Not yourn."

"Do it, or I will tell them you were with Ro today when she warned the Hatfields."

"I wasn't!"

She reached out to slap me. I ducked, but her hand caught my ear and I started to yowl.

"Hush, or you'll get more! Do as I say with the pebble. Now!"

"What will Ma say when she sees it there?" I sobbed.

"She'll figure Jesus put it there and decide that's where it should be. Now do it." She held the candle over the pebbles. I found mine, the smallest one because I was the youngest.

"Now put it on the side of the damned."

I did so. Only one other was there now. Ro's. *So,* I thought, *for all her talk Ma still thinks Ro is damned.* In the eerie light cast on the tree stump, Ro's and my pebbles looked awful lonesome, while on the other side all the other family pebbles kept each other company.

"You're damned for your lie," Alifair whispered to me. "Your covenant with God is broken. Suppose Johnse hadn't knocked that gun out of his father's hand? Pa would be dead. And it would be on your head. Don't lie anymore. Your sin will ride heavy on you and maybe even bring His wrath down on this house. Now go to bed and think on that."

I ran back to the house and to my room, where I jumped under the covers, all the time shivering. My sister was right, I was convinced of it. I'd betrayed my family. What if Johnse hadn't knocked the gun from his father's hand? I lay awake most of the night, tossing and turning, listening to the night wind and sounds outside my window. Once I smelled a skunk circling the house. And then I knew it wasn't a skunk. It was Yeller Thing, out there, waiting for me. Waiting to take me into the woods with him. Because he knew I deserved it.

I fell asleep just as the sky was turning gray in the east. I slept deeply. And then Alifair was standing over me again, this time fully dressed. "Fanny, get up. You've overslept."

My head ached like I had an ague. But I sat up. Sunlight hurt my eyes. I smelled coffee and frying ham.

She stood there with her hands on her hips. From the yard came loud voices. "The boys have sighted a visitor coming up the lane," she said with grim satisfaction. "Thought you'd want to be out there. You shouldn't miss this. It's Roseanna."

Numb with terror again, I got up and followed obediently.

Chapter Eighteen

FALL 1880

PHARMER, BUD, AND Bill were by the gate in the yard. Mama was at the doorstep. Adelaide and Trinvilla were in the kitchen garden in front. All frozen like some painting I'd seen in Bible lessons. Mama looked like Lot's wife standing there, like she was told not to look at Ro or she'd be turned into a pillar of salt. She wasn't looking. She was turned away, talking to Trinvilla about the beans in the garden.

I followed Alifair down the path to the gate and stood like a mule with colic, watching Ro come. She looked right smart in a new calico dress Aunt Betty had made her. And Clothilda had on a proper leather harness. At the gate she stopped, looked at everybody, and sort of smiled.

"Howdy," she said.

I started forward, but Alifair had a grip on my arm like a bear trap. "Let me *go*! You made me come out here, now let me go to her." I felt a panic rising inside me. Somehow I had to break free of my sister and keep Ro from coming to our gate. I knew that if she came through that gate harm would come to her. They had something planned, I felt it in my bones.

"Stay here and let the boys attend to her."

Attend to her? Alifair sounded like Mr. Cuzlin, like Ro was a contrary five-year-old. I fought her, but she hung on to my wrist. "Ma!" I called.

What did I expect? Ma quoted the Bible. "Your children will meet the enemy at the gates." She turned her mind again to those beans.

The enemy? Is that how she sees Ro now? Oh! I sobbed, then stopped fussing to watch my sister get down off Clothilda, come to the gate, and open it. Then Pharmer had his hand on it, holding it closed. "Afore you come in, Ro, there's something we've a mind to ask you."

I saw her look into Pharmer's face, then Bud's and Bill's. Ro wasn't stupid. What she saw there made her drop her hand from the gate. "Ask," she said.

"Did you ride off yesterday and tell the Hatfields that Pa and Jim had Johnse?"

Silence settled over the front yard. Ro's answer was so soft I couldn't hear it, but I didn't have to. Her head was bowed. I knew what she said.

"You mean you told those spawn of the Devil so's they'd come after Pa and Jim? What were you a-thinkin', Ro?"

I heard her sob. "Of Johnse. I didn't want them to shoot Johnse."

"Did Jim promise you he wouldn't?"

She nodded. "But Pa," she said, "it was Pa I was afeared would shoot him."

"So you told the Hatfields so they could shoot your own kin."

"I didn't think," she said. "I didn't think that far. I only thought to save Johnse."

"Well you should of," Pharmer said. "Now Pa isn't home, Ro. But as the oldest son here, I speak for him. You have to go. And not come back here again, you hear?"

I couldn't believe what Pharmer was saying! Not come back again? How could they! Again I struggled to free myself but couldn't. Ro looked up, wiping her eyes, staring around at the place like she'd never seen it before. She stared at Bud and Bill in turn, then at Adelaide and Trinvilla, who'd already turned to salt there in the garden. Her eyes went to Alifair, who was still holding me, to me, then to Ma. It was to Ma that she reached out her hand. "Mama?"

"You gotta go, Ro," Pharmer said. "Now. Sorry, but you can't see Ma. You sent Hatfields to kill her husband."

"I didn't!" Ro came to life then and pushed the gate open.

"Well, old Devil Anse was set to shoot Pa, and would of if Johnse didn't stop him."

"Then Johnse saved his life. What's wrong with you people? Why don't you bring a stop to all this?"

"You started it, Ro, when you ran off with Johnse. Now it's set its own course and it can't be stopped,"

Pharmer said. Then he closed the gate against her. The click of it sounded in the yard so loud I thought it would burst my eardrums. "Go, Ro, and don't come back. Ever."

"Ma," she called. "You can't mean this! You can't be sending me off like this!"

"But God shoots His arrows at conspirators. Suddenly they are struck. He brings them down by their own tongues." That was all Ma said. It was enough.

Ro's shoulders slumped. She turned to go. It was then that I bit Alifair's arm hard enough to make her yell and ran down the path to my sister. "Ro! Ro, wait, I'm coming," I yelled.

Bud and Bill tried to hold me, but I kicked them and fought like a painter cat.

"Leave her say good-bye," Pharmer said.

Bud and Bill obeyed, and I opened the gate and went through to Ro. I hugged her, smelled her glycerin and rosewater, felt the rise of her belly others did not know about.

"It's okay, baby," she said. "I'll be all right. Don't cry."

"I want to come with you."

"No, no, you stay here. Here's where you belong."

I couldn't see her face for my tears. "I'll come see you," I whispered. "I promise."

She nodded and smoothed my hair, tucked it behind my ears. I gave her one final hug and ran back through the gate. But I didn't run into the house. I ran around it, past the outbuildings, through the holler, across the creek, and into the woods toward my playhouse. My feet were bare. I felt the sharpness of rocks, twigs, underbrush, but I didn't care. Nothing could hurt me more than what they'd done to me this morning.

Before I climbed the ladder to the tree house, I stopped and looked around. I was all alone in the woods. Sunlight dappled through the colorful trees. A squirrel darted away when he saw me coming. From the distance some birds were chattering in the trees. Then of a sudden they stopped and it was silent, so silent all I could hear was the beating of my own heart.

And then I felt eyes watching me.

Yeller Thing! I felt the fear crawl up my throat. I felt it in my mouth, my arms, my legs. Fear so black and terrible it ate me up right there and spit me out. I wiped my face with my hands and looked around again.

Now I heard it, a faint hissing growl, like it was setting there watching me and getting ready to leap. Had he been here all along, knowing I'd come? Or had I conjured him?

And then something else happened. I was so all-fired mad at my family, at their stupidity, their meanness to Ro, that I didn't care if Yeller Thing was there waiting for me.

"Come on and get me!" I yelled. "Come on! I don't care!"

I screamed it in the silent woods. It echoed, bounced off the trees. The roosting birds took off in fright with a flurry of beating wings, flew away, and then it was silent again.

I waited, trembling, in my cotton nightdress and bare

feet. But Yeller Thing didn't come. I think if I'd of waited all day he wouldn't of come.

Coward, I thought. *Only fit to scare little girls.* And I climbed the steps to my playhouse. But inside myself I knew he was no coward. Settled in my safe spot, I knew that it just wasn't time yet for him to come, that was all. He wasn't ready yet. He had more plans for me. More terror for us all.

"Fanny? Hey, Fanny, you up there? Come on down, child. I'm here to take you home."

Tolbert! Was I dreaming? I'd fallen asleep! I sat up and crawled across the playhouse floor to look down. No, I wasn't dreaming. It was Tolbert, sitting on his horse right below, peering up at me.

"You in trouble with Alifair again?"

"She's meaner than a black bear, Tolbert. I hate her. And they sent Ro away for good. Did you know that? I hate all of 'em, and I'm not going home!"

"Not with me?"

I came full awake then. "I'm allowed?"

"Ma told as you and Alifair had a set-to; maybe it's best you spent some time with me, Mary, and Cora. I've got a bundle of your things. Well? You a-comin'? Or you aim to live in that tree house?"

So, for all her Bible-quoting, Ma did have her wits about her. And she'd sent for Tolbert, to get me away. From the ladder he grabbed me around the waist and set me in front of him on his horse. If Yeller Thing was still in those woods, let him come out now. I double dared him.

Chapter Nineteen

FALL 1880

BABY CORA TODDLED about on fat little legs, shaking her head and saying "no, no" when you told her she couldn't do something. I fed her, bathed her, combed her wispy baby hair, and I would have played with her all day if Tolbert didn't make me go to school.

I stayed a week with them. I was feeling more and more at home at their place. The house itself comforted me. The wood in the common room seemed to gleam in the firelight more than ours at home. Mary had a quilt on the wall over the settee. Ma would say quilts belonged only on beds. Their candles smelled good, and somehow the things they used to live every day—apples drying on a table, Mary's butter churn and spinning wheel, her bunches of herbs hanging overhead, Tolbert's bullet mold, his pelts hanging on the walls, the baby's cradle—looked purty lying about. Ours didn't at home.

Maybe it was only the play of the light, I told myself. The light seemed different here.

I especially liked Tolbert's books. He had lots of them. One was *Declaration of the Rights of Man*. One night when I was supposed to be doing my lesson I asked him, "What's 'rights'?"

He was molding bullets. "It's something God gives us that nobody can take. Rights to live and think free, worship, read, talk, have families and raise 'em the way you want. It's what our ancestors fought for in the Revolution."

"You always have to fight for rights?"

He smiled. "Most of the time, yes."

"Do only men have them?"

From a chair by the fire, doing mending, Mary spoke. "Well? Answer her, Tolbert."

But instead he smiled. "What do you want, Fanny?"

"I want to go visit Ro. I miss her and I'm afeared for her."

"Can't let you do that. Pa's got men in the woods with guns lest Johnse comes by. It's dangerous."

"You could come with me. It wouldn't be dangerous then."

Silence. He wiped his hands with a rag. His yellow hair gleamed in the firelight. I saw him look at Mary, saw the look on her face, like she was saying something without opening her mouth. Saw him nod to her. Then he said, "All right, I'll take you." And I knew that Mary had rights.

In bed that night I was so excited about seeing Ro

I could scarce sleep. The last thought I had before going off was, *Then didn't God give Johnse rights to wed Roseanna?*

TOLBERT TELLS THE best stories. On the way to Roseanna's we passed Granny Meeker's place, which is about two miles from Stringtown. She was limping around her yard and waved to Tolbert. He waved back. "Know why she limps?" he asked.

'Course I said no. So he told me. Said that she was a witch. And she put a spell on old Henry Crumley, who had a farm down the road. And to go about without he should see her, she changed herself into an old hen turkey.

"Well," Tolbert said, "Henry got vexed with this old hen turkey poking around his place and tried to shoot it. He shot lots of times and hit it, but it wouldn't die. So then a friend tells him that's because it's old Granny Meeker who turned herself into a hen turkey to plague him. And what he had to do was make himself a silver bullet and it'd kill her for sure. So Henry made himself a silver bullet and shot the hen turkey and it fell down dead. And the next time he saw old Granny Meeker she was limping around in her yard after a bad spell of sickness. And she never did bother him again."

"Do you think a silver bullet would kill Yeller Thing?" I asked him.

"If'n he'd stand still, maybe."

I pondered Tolbert's story on that ride to Aunt

Betty's. I knew about witches. A witch woman could ask to borrow something from you, and if you refused she could do you ill. Some people had witch marks over their doors to protect them. Ma said we didn't need one, Jesus would protect us.

I wondered if a silver bullet would kill Yeller Thing, if anything would. As it turned out, I should have been pondering other things. Soon's we got there, Tolbert saw that Ro was expecting. Of a sudden it seemed like you could tell. And it came to me that I hadn't told Tolbert. He didn't say anything, just went about his business of fixing Aunt Betty's door, while me and Ro visited.

She was working on the Coffin quilt. "Has Johnse been around?" I asked.

"No. Nobody's been here, Fanny." She sounded sad. "I'm a marked woman. Not only for the baby but because I set the Hatfields against our family. I'm worse now than Belle Beaver. But it's all right. Aunt Betty is good to me. And we've been making baby clothes. I'm happy here. My baby will be born in March, and I'll have my little one to love."

"But don't you miss Johnse?"

She lowered her eyes, not looking at me. "I told him I won't marry him, Fanny."

What had happened in the past weeks? I just stared at her.

"All it'll lead to is killing," she said. "You heard how Devil Anse almost killed Pa. I don't want my baby marked by such doings." She was set on it and would speak of it no more. So we made small talk and soon the visit was over. There was no sign of Pa's men watching the place.

I promised to come again. But before we left, Tolbert pulled me aside. "She's a-havin' a little 'un," he said. And he looked at me as if it was my fault.

I nodded.

"How long you known?"

"Since before she left home. I wanted to tell you, but I couldn't. She swore me not to. Please don't be mad, Tolbert."

He hooked his thumbs in his back pockets and stared over my head to Ro. "You stay here tonight," he said quietly.

Tears came to my eyes. "You mean you don't want me with you and Mary anymore?"

"Don't be silly, Fanny. I want you to stay here because I'm a-goin' home and tellin' Ma."

He was walking to his horse. I ran after him and grabbed his arm. "You can't! Ro doesn't want Ma to know." I hung on his arm.

"Fanny," he said, "I wasn't angry, but I'm a-gettin' there. I don't care what Ro wants. I care about this family. I care about what's right. Ma would want to know, and you know it. Now let go."

I let go. "I don't have any clothes with me," I said.

"You can manage. I'll be back tomorrow with Ma. You stay here and wait, you hear?"

"What if Pa goes after Johnse with guns?"

He swung up onto his horse. "I want to find you

here tomorrow, Fanny," was all he said. "And don't tell Ro, either. It'll work out, don't worry."

I wish I could say it all worked out. I wish I could end this account here and say the baby made a difference. Oh, it did with Ma. Like Tolbert said, he brought her back the next day. She came to see Ro, and they hugged and cried and sat and had cups of tea and talked like God was in His heaven and all was right with the world, the way women do when it has to do with babies. But nobody else came, and Pa never sent word.

I went back home. Fall deepened. The nights got colder, though some days were still warm. We brought out the blankets. My brothers stacked the wood by the door. Alifair was off to a revival meeting for two weeks so I was free of her. I helped Ma make apple butter. We went to a corn shucking. In church they were getting ready for the Christmas pageant and I was asked to be part of it. But all I could think of when they talked about Mary, and how as she didn't have a place to birth her baby, was Ro. And how there was no room for her at our house. Or at Devil Anse's. I said no to the Christmas pageant. Nancy McCoy played Mary. I sang in the choir. The songs gave me comfort.

At Christmas I brought a special basket to Belle Beaver. She asked after Ro and I lied and told her, yes, I'd given her the comb and she loved it. "These people around here ain't the forgivin' kind," she told me. "She ought to take her feller and move away."

I wished it could be so simple. In March, the end of a

bitter winter, Ro had a baby girl. Only Aunt Betty attended her, though I went with Ma to see her. Ma was beside herself with joy. Ro's joy was quiet and tinged with sadness.

"A darlin' little baby," Ma said. "Looks just like you, Ro." Aunt Betty agreed.

The baby had blond hair, not dark like my sister's. Was everybody blind? Couldn't they see it looked just like Johnse?

Chapter Twenty

DECEMBER 1881

RO'S BABY, LITTLE Sarah Elizabeth, loved me. She was only nine months in December, but Ro said she looked for my coming. When I did come she wanted only me, clung to me and stared at me with her big blue eyes as if I was somebody special. It made me all weak and mushy inside. I hated leaving her.

"Your sister's in a little paradise all her own," Aunt Betty told me. "And I feel like a grandmother. I'm enjoying it a heap, I can tell you."

I envied Ro, living in her cottony world, but the world outside went on, meaner than ever. I didn't tell her, of course. But neighbors gossiped about her and the baby, saying it was "conceived in sin," that it had the hated Hatfield blood. On the other side of the coin, word came to us that Devil Anse was sorry he hadn't allowed Johnse to wed Roseanna. He'd heard about the cunning baby and was going around bragging that it had his blood. But now it was too late.

"Too late, why?" I asked Ma. But she only shook her head and didn't say.

One day right before Christmas I lingered after school to help straighten up instead of going to Ro's, because Sarah Elizabeth had the measles. Ma had been there for two days now. I had the jimjams because I wasn't allowed to go. I hadn't had measles yet. All I could think of was little Sarah Elizabeth. Was she looking for me?

Nancy McCoy lingered after school, too, but she wasn't helping. That's when she told me that Johnse was a-carousin' and drinking. "And seeking solace at Belle Beaver's place."

"What for?" I asked.

She grinned. "Well, it isn't for maple candy. It's such a shame, a nice boy like Johnse going to Belle for solace. She should be told to leave him be and maybe he'd wed who he wanted."

Why was she taking up for Roseanna of a sudden? Then I decided that though Nancy was a low-down slithering snake, maybe she was right. Maybe all that had to be done was tell Belle to turn Johnse away so's he could think how much he loved Roseanna. He'd only been once to see the baby. That's what he needed, to visit again and see that adorable child.

Ma had got up a big basket of vittles for Belle and I was to take it on the twenty-second. I thought it brave of Ma. Other church ladies were all in a huff about Belle. It seemed like a lot of their menfolk were visiting her again, so they'd sent a delegation to my brother Jim, who said he'd ponder it. Jim never did anything without he pondered it well. And I know he told Tolbert and Mary that it wasn't right to turn a woman out of her home in the snows of winter.

A fresh layer of snow had fallen the night before, but it hardly counted as the snows of winter. It was powdery. And it glistened in the morning sun. On my way to school I felt good lugging Belle's basket. On this visit I'd talk to Belle, tell her about Ro's beautiful baby and how maybe she could turn Johnse away when he next came to see her. Adelaide and Trinvilla walked on ahead, making snowballs and throwing them at each other.

A thin wisp of smoke curled up out of Belle Beaver's chimney. I hurried down her narrow path and knocked on the patched-up door. Usually she came right out, but now she didn't. I knocked again. There was a muffled sound from inside. I pushed the door open and dropped the basket. A jar of molasses and a ham rolled onto the floor. I stood there and screamed.

Belle was hanging from the rafters. *Buck naked*. And dead.

I turned to run, but a cry stopped me, and then her feet started to wiggle. She was alive! And then I saw she wasn't altogether naked, but that her print dress was pulled up and tied around her neck. Cloth was stuffed in her mouth. *I had to do something! But what?*

She was mumbling through the rag in her mouth and casting her eyes in the direction of a small bench. I crossed the room to seize it. More muffled cries. She was shaking her head no. Why? Oh. She was now looking to a table where a bowl and cup and some utensils were laid out. And I understood. There was a large, ugly knife. Of course. She wanted me to cut the rope.

I grabbed the knife, dragged over the small bench, and climbed onto it, but when I reached up I could not reach the rope binding her to the rafters. I couldn't even reach the gag in her mouth.

I must get help, I thought. The fire in the old stone fireplace was fast fading, the place was freezing cold. I jumped down from the bench. "I'm going for help. The school is closer than my brother Tolbert's house. I'll be back soon." Before I left I threw a log on the fire.

I ran all the rest of the way to school. I heard Mr. Cuzlin ringing the old school bell before I even got through the woods, saw him walking back across the snow-covered yard to the school. I'd been running so fast I could scarce find my breath, but I stopped and yelled, "Mr. Cuzlin!"

He turned, saw me, and waved.

Right about then I slipped and fell and he started toward me. By the time he reached me I was on my feet, but tears were frozen on my face. There's no telling what the poor man thought, seeing me all out of breath and crying like that. Likely that I was chased by a black bear.

No matter. When he heard what misery I was toting, he turned to one of the older girls who was just coming into the schoolyard, told her to take charge, and came with me back to Belle's.

WE CUT HER down and took the gag from her mouth. She was dazed and freezing. We got her dress straightened. Mr. Cuzlin was so embarrassed by her state that he didn't look at me. Just gave orders. "Fetch that brandy over there. Make her a cup of tea and get that comforter." I did as I was told. Then he told me to build up the fire and I did that, too. I picked up Ma's vittles, which were all over the floor, and put them in the cupboard.

When Mr. Cuzlin asked her who did this to her, she shook her head and couldn't speak at first. I confess that for a minute I held my breath, hoping it wasn't my brother Jim. But inside me I knew that Jim didn't mistreat women, even those labeled "bad."

"Don't know," she said. "They had their faces covered. But they were young. Said they'd had enough of my evil ways and wanted me out of their God-lovin' community. Said I should stop corruptin' the likes of young Johnse Hatfield. Said their sister and him was a-fixin' to wed."

I felt my face go hot. "It wasn't my brothers," I said. "They wouldn't do such."

He said nothing.

It wasn't, I wanted to scream. But who wanted their sister to wed Johnse Hatfield?

"Like I invited that Johnse feller here," she was saying. "I ask you, sir, is this the work of God? What they did to me? Well, I'm a-leavin'. Belle doesn't want any truck with a place where the men don't treat women like ladies, even if'n I don't go to church. I'm leavin' tonight."

"More snow is on the way," Mr. Cuzlin told her. "Might be you should wait a spell. You know how the snow gets in these mountains."

"I'll take my chances with the snow and the mountains afore I take my chances with these God-fearin' people," she told him.

We stayed with her a bit until she was herself again. Then we left. I went out the door first, as I was told, but when I turned to close it behind me I saw Mr. Cuzlin hand her some money. "In case you need it."

On the way back to school again, I defended my brothers. "They don't even want Johnse to wed Ro," I told him. I found that I cared what he thought, dearly.

He nodded. "Somebody could just be throwing the blame on your brothers," he said to me. By the time we got back to school it was near noon. Nancy McCoy had taken charge.

"Don't you think I've done a good job?" she asked. Her eyes flirted with him.

"I think you have done a complete job," he told her. "And you have gotten your way."

I did not take his meaning. But Nancy did. She flounced to her seat. Soon I found that everybody in the schoolroom knew where we'd been and wanted to know if Belle Beaver was dead. Then I knew who had attacked Belle Beaver. But why? Oh, I didn't know. My feet were so cold, and the sight of Belle hanging naked was frozen somewhere inside me forever.

On the way home when I passed her place I saw that

she was gone. The door swung open, banging in the winter wind. There was no more smoke from the chimney. Ahead of me on the path I heard Adelaide and Trinvilla giggling. "Too bad," Adelaide said. "Now the only bad woman left in these parts for people to talk about is our own sister."

I caught up with Adelaide, gave her a good smack, and kept running. I'd be punished when I got home by Alifair, but I didn't care. When I got home, though, there was no punishment. There was only Alifair waiting to tell us that she'd had word from Ma. Ro's baby had gotten pneumonia from the measles. And died. I dropped my books and ran all the way to Aunt Betty's.

Chapter Twenty-One

DECEMBER 1881–JANUARY 1882

PA HAD NEVER seen Roseanna's baby girl, but now he stood with us on a knoll behind Aunt Betty's place when they put the little coffin Floyd had made into the cold ground.

My heart was near ruined. Sometimes I thought it wasn't even there anymore inside me. All that was there when I reached was a hollow ache.

Little Sarah Elizabeth dead! I couldn't believe it. Nobody died from measles! But what haunted me most was, did she look for me to come and see her? Was she waiting? Did she wonder why I hadn't come?

My brothers covered the casket with earth. When that was done, Pa went over to Roseanna and said something soft in her ear. It was the first time he'd spoken to her since she came home after her stay with the Hatfields. Ro's face didn't change at all. She didn't even act like Pa spoke. I don't think she was being ornery. I just think Ro didn't know where she was or who was with her. I think she was in someplace all her own, out of reach of us all.

———

I FOUND OUT later that Pa invited Ro to come and stay with us for a spell, but she refused. She went home with Aunt Betty and our lives went on. In our house things were quiet. Nobody spoke of the baby or Ro. But not speaking of them was worse. It was like they were there in the room with us and we kept tripping over them all the time.

I wished it was summer so I could stay in my play-house. I wished I could go to Mary and Tolbert's. I did go to Aunt Betty's a lot to see my sister, but I'd just as lief as stayed home. Ro didn't talk to me. Most of the time she wasn't even in the house. She was out in the cold, on that knoll, sitting in the snow at the baby's grave. And no kind of talk or tears could bring her around.

———

JOHNSE HATFIELD HADN'T come to the funeral. Everybody thought that was just the awfulest thing, that he didn't show to put his own baby girl into the ground. Nobody gave much mind to the fact that my pa might kill him if he showed. They just went around mouth-ing bad things about Johnse. The stories got better every day, too. We heard he'd run off to follow Belle Beaver. Another story said he'd gone to Florida to do blacksmithing. Still another held that he'd been wandering around in the mountains and was attacked by a bear.

And then one day, the first cold week in January, he was there, outside our schoolroom, on his horse. All bundled up in the cold and waiting.

I saw him from the window and for a minute it was as much of a jolt as seeing Yeller Thing. What was he doing here at our school? Had something happened now to Ro? Was he here to tell me? I could scarce wait to get outside. But then Mr. Cuzlin wanted to tell me something about my ciphering. By the time I got outside, he was off his horse and talking with Nancy McCoy. And while I stood there like a jackass in the rain, he helped Nancy up onto his horse, climbed up behind her, and they rode away.

It came to me then. I'd forgotten about this, what with all the sadness of Ro's baby dying. I'd forgotten about the day when me and Mr. Cuzlin had cut Belle Beaver down and she'd said some men had tied her up, some men who wanted Johnse to wed their sister. It wasn't my brothers. I knew that for certain. And I recollected how, when we got back to the schoolroom that day, everybody knew where we'd been and what had happened to Belle. And what Mr. Cuzlin said to Nancy.

It was Nancy McCoy's brothers then, who got rid of Belle Beaver. And now, soon as it was decent after his baby died, here was Johnse Hatfield, come a-courtin' Nancy McCoy. Because courting was what it was. There was no other name you could put on it.

He came every day after that, good weather or bad.

Every day just as we were finishing up in the afternoon I'd look out the window and there he'd be. All bundled in the January cold—gloves, scarf, everything, even an extra blanket to wrap about Nancy, who rushed out soon's she was given leave. She came every day to school now, too. Middle of winter lots of kids didn't come. Some were sickly. We'd heard there was some ailment going around that sounded like typhoid. Some parents were afeared to let their children come to school. Other young 'uns just didn't have warm enough clothes. Still others didn't bother coming through the snow. But Nancy came.

You couldn't keep a thing like that secret, of course. My two big-mouth sisters told Alifair about it the first day, then Alifair went off to another of her healing meetings for a week and soon everybody was pondering it wherever you went.

Johnse Hatfield had himself another McCoy woman. How could he? Didn't he have the sense God gave a goose? Weren't there enough purty women over to West Virginia? Did he have to cross the river to Kentucky to find one?

Oh, people were all fired up, talking about it. *Why didn't Nancy's brothers stop him?*

"How can he wed her when Ro just lost her baby?" Alifair asked. She was home from her healing group, looking wan and saying she was stronger in the Lord and filled with the light of holiness. For once I was in agreement with her about Ro. Especially when she added, "How can Johnse stand up to his pa about Nancy when he couldn't stand up to him about Ro?"

My own brothers were so fired up they were ready to ride out and tar and feather Johnse. Calvin went to visit Nancy. He talked with her brother Lark and came back and told us Lark liked Johnse, though Nancy's mother was going about the house slamming things when Johnse came to call. That was all Ma needed. She took herself off to visit Nancy's ma and stayed the whole day. I don't think she cared if Nancy married old Lucifer himself. She was doing it for Ro.

She came home grimfaced and sat down to table. We all waited. "Nancy's ma would rather see Nancy dead than wed to Johnse," she told us. "But she can't do a thing with Nancy, she's so spoilt. Lark is the oldest and he's taken up for her. He says it weren't Johnse's fault he didn't wed Ro. It was yourn, Ranel. And Devil Anse's. He says that Johnse is determined to wed Nancy and not let his pa interfere this time. Lark said he's a-goin' with them when they ask Devil Anse."

It went on all through the end of January and into February. Nancy kept coming to school and Johnse kept coming to fetch her after. People were saying no good would come of it, that Johnse was touched by the Devil and after what had happened to Ro and the baby he ought to be run out of Kentucky. But what could anybody do if Lark wouldn't stop them?

Then, at the end of February, Johnse Hatfield wed Nancy McCoy over in West Virginia. Calvin found out that Lark had gone with Johnse and Nancy to get Devil Anse's blessing, that Nancy had stood up to Devil Anse, who said he liked her "spark" and agreed to it.

The wedding quieted things down. Some folk from

Kentucky even went across the river to help build the cabin for Johnse and Nancy. None of my brothers went.

Johnse and Nancy moved in in March, the day my sister Alifair came down sick with the typhoid.

Chapter Twenty-Two

MARCH 1882

I LAY IN my bed in the dark while the March winds howled outside our house. Was that sound the wind? Or my sister Alifair howling? Might be it was Yeller Thing out there. Or all three.

"She a-goin' to die?" Trinvilla asked me. I didn't know which was worse—Alifair's yelling or having Trinvilla and Alelaide in the room with me for two days now. They couldn't be near Alifair. The doctor had come and gone, a rare occasion in these parts, and pronounced Alifair's sickness typhoid. The reason he was gone so quick was that a lot of families in the mountains had it. He couldn't tarry.

"I don't know," I said. I was in no mood to comfort my sisters. Now that Alifair was down sick they turned to me.

"She wouldn't die if Ma'd let me give her remedies,"

Adelaide said, "or sent for Aunt Cory instead of the old doctor."

More screaming. Alifair was what the doctor had called "delirious." Ma called it "out of her head." She kept yelling for Roseanna. "Roseanna, Roseanna, forgive me!"

"Nothing Ro has to forgive her for," Adelaide mumbled now in the dark.

"Well, she's out of her head, but she knows more than you," I told her.

"Why can't Alifair heal herself?" Trinvilla asked. "She goes to all those healing groups."

A good question. The great healer was sick. Where was her light of holiness now? Her power? I did not feel sorry for her. I just wished she'd stop yelling. I was getting a headache. "Ma will be down sick next," I said, "if she doesn't get some rest." For two days and nights now Ma hadn't taken to her bed for sleep.

"Will she die?" Trinvilla asked again. "I couldn't abide it if she died."

"Hush!" I said sternly. How many times had I wished Alifair dead? And with good reason. If she died now would the fault be mine?

More howling wind outside. It was still very cold. At that moment the bedroom door opened and Calvin stood there, all dressed, though it was near the middle of the night.

"Fanny, get up and dressed, quicklike. We're goin' to fetch Roseanna. Ma says if she comes, might be Alifair will get on the mend."

I sat up and stared at him, backlit from a lantern in the hall. "This time of night?"

"Now," he said again. "Be quick about it and dress warm. I'll fetch the horses."

———

IT WAS WEEKS before we knew Alifair wouldn't die. And from the night me and Calvin knocked on Aunt Betty's door and a light appeared behind the window and Ro started throwing clothes on, she didn't need convincing to come home. Alifair was took sick. It was enough. As we rode through the March night all she asked of Calvin was how bad Alifair was and what the doctor had said. *How can she care?* I asked myself. Alifair had been nothing but mean to her since the whole business with Johnse began. It was a part of Ro I could not understand. I supposed it was the part that had loved a man and had his baby. And buried it on a knoll behind the hill.

I wanted to understand, but I couldn't. Ever since the death of her baby, Ro was someplace inside her I couldn't go.

When we got home, she ran right in to help Ma, like she'd never been away. Times she slept, she settled right into her old bed in our room, though she didn't sleep that much. Trinvilla and Adelaide were put in the parlor.

I wasn't allowed in Alifair's room, but I stood outside and saw Ro run to her, saw Alifair reach out her arms, saw them embrace. For many a night after that I woke to find Ro's bed empty. I'd get up to walk out into the hall, and there I'd see the shadow of Ro on the wall in Alifair's room, cast larger than life by a lantern. Nothing seemed real anymore. People moved about the house at night. Alifair continued to moan and thrash. Ma prayed aloud and walked around like she was under a spell. I worried that Ro would get the typhoid. Who would tend her? What would I do if she died?

Pa and the boys stayed out of the house as much as they could. They were doing the spring planting. Adelaide did the cow milking. Trinvilla washed the dishes. I cooked. I was somewhat of a fair hand at it. Tolbert's wife, Mary, let me help when I visited. Alifair never would at home. I made a right smart venison stew, too, though Calvin had to cut up the meat for me. I was a fair hand at quail, too. My brothers brought in two and I rubbed them all over with butter, salt, and pepper and put them in a pan until they got nice and brown in our stove oven. Mary kept us in fresh-baked bread and pies. Nobody complained about my cooking. Nobody complained or fussed very much about anything.

What seemed to be happening, if you put your mind to it, was that we were all getting along in our house, helping each other. We talked in soft tones. Even Trinvilla and Adelaide behaved and told me my cooking was near as good as Ma's.

Did we have to have death at the door, I wondered, for us to get on?

But most of all was the change in Ro. She'd come to us pale and in mourning. In the weeks in which she nursed Alifair color came to her cheeks. She was eating, something Aunt Betty had said she hadn't done since the baby died. She was filled with purpose.

Pa didn't talk to her, no. He never said one word to her face. But neither did he bad-mouth her. They just sort of moved around each other real careful-like.

One day after he'd been to Pikeville, Calvin handed Ro a note. She read it and shoved it into her apron pocket. Nobody asked about it. But I think everybody was hoping it wasn't from Johnse.

"Fanny," Ro told me in our room that night, "for the first time since little Sarah died I feel I have a reason for living. Soon's Alifair is on the mend I'm a-goin' to Martha Cline's over to Pikeville. She's got six little 'uns and they got the typhoid. She's asked me to come and help her tend 'em."

"Suppose you get sick?" I asked.

"I won't."

"How can you be sure?"

" 'Cause I don't care if I die, Fanny baby. And God don't take people like that. It means that living for such a person is a worse punishment. And God wants me to be punished."

"Why?"

"Why, for what I did to this family," she said simply. "For the way it's tore us apart. We're all tore apart, Fanny. And that's another reason I can't stay."

She left the third week in April to attend Martha Cline's family. And she didn't get typhoid. And she never once spoke of Nancy being wed to Johnse Hatfield.

Alifair recovered. We went back to school. I thought it an oddment that Alifair, with all her powers and her healing meetings, had needed Ro, a sinner, to make her well. But nobody else thought of it. And soon's Alifair was up and about she was back in the kitchen taking over and bossing me around, mean as a hornet all over again. Once, when she found out I hadn't scrubbed a certain pot after using it, she even hit me.

"I wish you'd a-died!" I shouted at her and ran out of the house.

Nobody cared that she hit me. Things were back to the way they always were.

Chapter Twenty-Three

AUGUST 1882

IF PEOPLE HEREABOUTS recollect Election Day of 1880 as the day my sister Roseanna ran off with Johnse Hatfield, they will always mark Election Day of 1882 as the time of the Big Trouble. The day commenced with a heavy morning mist that everybody said would burn off and become heat. They were right. The heat lay on us all. So did the bugs and the mood of trouble. Because the Hatfields were coming.

The past summer had been quiet, with nobody fussing at anybody, but underneath you could sense that everybody was just a-waitin' for some trouble they couldn't put a name to. If we get through Election Day we'll be right as rain, they were a-sayin'. Everybody knew Devil Anse and his kin were coming. That put the hex on Election Day, of course, and made everybody nervous as an ugly girl at a box-supper auction.

I was nine then and old enough to get a purchase on

the feeling. The end of August is a bad time anyways. People are tuckered out from the summer farm work, the harvest is still not yet in, and they're strung tighter than a fiddle string about to break for too much pluckin'. My brother Floyd was the first to alert me.

I was up at his cabin because I was to help him bring his whiskey and toys. Right off I saw he was loading no whiskey into the wagon, but I didn't ask why. Instead I asked why Devil Anse and his people were even allowed to come to our elections.

"Don't they have their own elections in West Virginny?"

It was then that Floyd told me why they'd always come. "Old Devil Anse tries to run things in Pike County elections. Why you think one of the officers in our sheriff's department is a Hatfield? Devil Anse buys votes. And this year he's boating his own whiskey across the Tug. Warned me not to bring mine. If that don't rile me, I don't know what."

"Did you tell Pa?"

" 'Course not. Ain't we had enough trouble? What trouble comes this year won't be on my account."

Everybody turned out. Everybody excepting Johnse and Nancy Hatfield and my sister Ro, of course. I missed Ro something awful. And I stayed on my lone most of the time, not joining in the kid games. After all, I was nine now, tall for my age, and I'd toted a lot of miseries. I was nobody's toady to be told to run a sack race or play toss and catch.

Watching the little kids play their games, I thought about my sister Ro. She was an oddment, that was a given. There was Adelaide still studying to be a granny lady and Alifair still going to meetings to heal people, and without any of their foolishness, Ro was going around regular-like now and taking care of sick people, wherever they were. She was so busy, I scarce saw her these days.

Elections went on normal enough that day, with Hatfields at one end of the field and McCoys at the other. In the middle was the dance platform. My brother Bill commenced to play "Sourwood Mountain," and right off Tolbert started in a-dancin'. Nobody could dance like Tolbert. Everybody clapped for him and told him to dance some more. Right then Black Elias Hatfield, brother of Devil Anse, stepped onto the platform and started running his mouth. They called him Black Elias because he always dressed all in black.

"Ain't there room for a Hatfield on this dance floor?" he asked.

"Soon's you pay me the five bucks you owe me, Lias," Tolbert said.

Lias got all stiff then, like he had a bone in his throat. "What money's that?" he asked my brother. And right off you could tell they weren't talking about money, that money was the last thing they were talking about. But Tolbert went on to remind him about the debt. Lias just laughed, of course, and said how Tolbert should try to come and get it from him, which around these parts is spoiling for a fight even if you aren't a Hatfield or a McCoy. Everybody backed off, the music stopped, and mamas started grabbing their children.

Tolbert and Lias went at each other like a coon dog

and a possum. Men in back of the crowd were taking bets. Lias was bigger than my brother, but he was drunk on Hatfield whiskey, and soon he was laid out on the dance platform. The Hatfields didn't cotton to this at all, naturally, and soon Elias's brother Ellison stepped onto the platform, and more insults were traded as these two had at it. Some women screamed as blood was drawn on both sides.

I got afeared for Tolbert. He was all wore out. Finally Ellison got a hold on him, one of those holds that could break a person's neck. Everybody in the crowd gasped. But then, quicker than a june bug, Tolbert got a knife from somewhere on his person and started slashing at Ellison, who would have killed him then and there if he could.

My brother Bill rushed onto the platform and started slashing Ellison, too. There was blood all over the place. I saw my brother Jim standing there watching, but he made no move to stop it.

From somewhere way behind me I heard Ma's voice praying.

Even though he was cut up like a hog on butchering day, Ellison landed Tolbert a blow on the head that knocked him flat. Tolbert lay still. Then Ellison grabbed up a piece of log from the end of the platform and raised it to dash Tolbert's brains out, but Pharmer stepped up with his Smith and Wesson and fired.

The shot echoed like the sound of God's fist. Everybody screamed, then got real quietlike. Tolbert bestirred himself, got up, and stood, real wobbly. Then Mary came and took him off the platform, just before Devil Anse

Hatfield stepped up and bent over his wounded brother. Devil Anse near went crazy then. He started shaking like he had the palsy, reached for his gun, and fired at Pharmer. He missed, and that made him even crazier. He cussed up a storm and grabbed Pharmer. But afore you know it, John Hatfield, who was a sheriff's officer just like Jim, grabbed Pharmer and arrested him.

"I'm a-takin' ye to the jail in Pikeville," he said.

Next thing you know, Tolbert broke away from Mary and came to stand with Pharmer.

"Where's t'other one?" John Hatfield asked. He directed his question at the crowd, but nobody answered.

My brother Jim then decided it was time to act. "I'm senior officer," he told Hatfield, "and I'll take 'em in hand."

But the Hatfield sheriff's man would have none of it. "Do ye think, Jim, that I'll turn McCoys over to you? Now where's t'other one?"

Then somebody was dragging my brother Bud over. "I didn't do anything," he was saying.

Bill came forward. "T'weren't Bud, it was me," he said. By now that Hatfield officer was so confused he couldn't have told a bear from a bobcat. He started in asking the crowd who did the knifing, Bill or Bud, while Jim stood there, grim and waiting.

But nobody knew. Bill and Bud looked too much alike. Some people allowed that it was Bud, so Officer Hatfield took Bud and left Bill standing there with his mouth open.

"I'm a-goin' along with you all," Jim said. Then my brothers Sam and Floyd said they were going, too.

Officer Hatfield looked like he had all he could handle. He didn't object.

"Pa McCoy, don't let them take them," Mary begged.

"No need to worry, Mary," he said. "No Kentucky jury will convict a McCoy for killing a Hatfield. And I'm a-ridin' into Pikeville now to get a lawyer."

He rode off. The crowd separated, mumbling and carrying pieces of the fight home with them, like the ham and chicken in their baskets. They would feed on it for a long time.

"It's not a jury or lawyers I'm worried about," Mary told me. "It's those darned fool Hatfields. They'll kill those three. Doesn't anybody know it?"

"Jim's with them," I reminded her.

She put her hand on my shoulder. "How would you like to come home with me tonight, Fanny?" she asked. "Keep me company, please."

I asked Ma and she said yes, so I went along with Mary. The sun was setting, but in the woods it was already dark with shadows as we hurried along with baby Cora. Mary wrung her hands and worried, and I comforted her. It would be all right, I said over and over, Jim was with them. But I knew it wasn't all right. I knew it true before we got to Mary's house.

'Cause there in the darkened woods, rushing around and hissing, I saw Yeller Thing.

Chapter Twenty-Four

AUGUST 1882

I COULDN'T RECOLLECT the last time I saw him. Times there were I'd forgotten him, forgotten to look for him in the woods. I couldn't recollect the last time I'd bothered to make a cross in the dirt with my toe, spit in it, and make a good wish before I left the house.

I'd come to think of Yeller Thing as something from my childhood that I had outgrown. But there he was, slinking and stinking around us as we made our way to Mary and Tolbert's house. Greenish yellow and shining with some unearthly glow. Waiting for me. I could feel him looking at me even though I knew he only had holes where those eyes should be. I could feel the slimy breeze he made as he circled around me, breathing and waiting.

Mary didn't see him, of course. So I acted brave and clutched her hand, pretending I was giving her comfort and not that she was giving it to me.

NEXT MORNING SHE woke me at first light, bundled up baby Cora, and we walked to our house. "We'll have breakfast there," she said. She was scared. She needed kinfolk.

There was a strange yellow cast to the air that morning. Something brooded over our house. I felt chilled in the August heat and sat next to the stove in the kitchen.

Pa was still in Pikeville, getting a lawyer for the boys. He'd wait there with the lawyer, Ma said, for the boys to be delivered there today by the sheriff's officers.

Alifair served breakfast. A few times I caught her looking at Mary with something in her eyes I couldn't name. Like she knew things. Like Yeller Thing, I minded. Alifair had toned down some since her typhoid, but hate still brewed in her like the whiskey in Floyd's still. And she stirred it all the time, the way you're supposed to so it won't go bad.

I knew she still hated me, and I still hated her. But she hadn't held my head under the pump of late, though she still gave me the rough side of her tongue regularlike. I had the feeling that she was saving up all her hatred for one fine moment.

Calvin was outside with Bill, doing the chores. We all knew, I think, that Pa should have been home from Pikeville already, that Pharmer, Bud, and Tolbert should have been delivered safely there to the jail. Funny the things we talked about. A new dress Ma was making for Alifair, how much soap we needed to make for the winter. At one point Alifair dropped a knife and we all jumped like a cannon went off. And Alifair got vexed with Ma for mumbling her prayers.

"There's a time for eating and a time for praying, Ma," she snapped. "Eat. You may need your strength."

Ma looked up as if she was disturbed from a dream. "What will I need my strength for?"

"Nothing," Alifair said. But she said it too quicklike. And again I felt that she knew something, that maybe her powers were working. "Nothing, Ma. Just pray if you want. I'm sorry."

Next thing we heard a horse ride up and everybody stopped eating. "Must be Pa," Ma said. And we all got up and went outside. It was not Pa. It was brother Jim. Calvin and Bill had come out of the barn and he was standing there talking to them real softlike. They turned and looked as the door slammed behind us. And nobody spoke for a minute. Jim looked abashed, like he'd just got caught stealing molasses candy.

"Tell me," Ma said.

I could see that if Jim had his druthers he'd have died first. "They been taken, Ma. Never got to Pikeville. About forty Hatfields rode up yesterday and took 'em off. Out-gunned us."

"Where?"

"West Virginny."

Mary gave a little scream and set down baby Cora. She started toward Jim, but Ma held her back. "Why West Virginny when this is a Kentucky fuss?"

"Devil Anse wants 'em in hand. Until he knows for sure that Ellison won't die."

"And if he dies?"

Jim shrugged. "T'weren't nothing we could do, Ma. Officer Hatfield didn't want to give 'em up any more than me or Sam or Floyd."

"So what do we do now?" Ma asked.

"I'm on my way," Jim said, "to get Pa. We'll round up some McCoys and go fetch 'em home from West Virginny."

"No!" Ma near shouted it. "No, Jim, it'll only mean killing. No more killing! The just man is glad in the Lord and takes refuge in Him."

"Ma," Jim said softly, "Psalms will be no help. It's men we need. McCoys with guns."

"If you go in with McCoys, they'll kill my boys!"

"If we don't go in they'll kill 'em anyways."

Another muffled moan from Mary.

"But others will fall!" Ma wailed. "Hasn't there been enough strife between us?"

"I don't care about others," Jim said. "I care about my brothers. I'm a-goin', Ma."

She ran to him. She grabbed his arm and turned him to face her. "No, Jim, wait. I beg you. Let me go!"

"You?"

"I'll go face down Devil Anse myself. I'll beg for my boys' lives. He won't hurt me."

"Ma, McCoys don't beg Hatfields for anything," Jim told her.

But she was already started back in the house. "You give me this chance, Jim. You promise me you'll wait until I've had this chance. I'm your own ma. You've got to heed me."

Jim was lost and he knew it.

"The Lord'll set a place for me at the table in the midst of my enemies," Ma said.

"I'll go with you, Ma," Jim said.

"No! No McCoy men and no guns. Just me and maybe Mary."

"Yes," Mary said, "yes. I'll go, Ma McCoy." She grabbed my arm. "And I'll bring baby Cora and Fanny. A delegation of women. How can old Devil Anse turn us down?"

———

LOOKING BACK ON it now, I see that I shouldn't have done it. I was old enough to know Ma was crazier than a hooty owl. I should have said no, I'm not going. Let Jim go get Pa. One of us should have had some sense. And I think if I'd said no, it would have made Mary stop and think, too. It was my place to say no. Ma was off somewhere, thinking of that place the Lord was going to set for her at the table in the midst of her enemies. Maybe already seeing that linen cloth and shiny silver. Mary only wanted to see Tolbert; baby Cora was too young. It was up to me and I went along with it. Because I was so honored to be asked. So glad to be part of it all. I sailed into the house, right past Alifair, who glared at me like she wanted to hold my head under the pump, and I made ready to go.

Baby Cora rode in front of me on the horse. I can still feel her warm sturdy little body against mine, hear the way she said, "Goin' to see Da Da." I think I shall always hear it.

At the Mate Creek Schoolhouse across the Tug,

Devil Anse greeted us like some ancient god, gray beard flowing, dressed in a black suit and hat. A perfect gentleman he was, helping Ma down from her horse, chucking baby Cora under the chin, and explaining how he was just holding the boys until he could be sure Ellison wouldn't die.

"And if he does?" Ma asked.

"Then we'll escort 'em back to Kentucky, to the jail," he promised. "Just want to make sure they don't escape between now and then is all."

"Mr. Hatfield, don't you think it's time this foolishment stopped between our families?"

"Mrs. McCoy," he returned, "it never would have started if your Roseanna hadn't run off with my boy. It's what this grew out of."

There it was between us.

"I held off my Jim from rounding up McCoys. That shows my heart is in the right place."

"If McCoys attack, your boys would be the first ones dead."

"I'll keep my men away if you promise to keep my boys alive," Ma said.

"No," Mary put in. "No, Ma, please. Don't promise. And don't beg."

Ma told her to hush. And she picked up baby Cora herself and carried her into the schoolhouse, proud, like we were walking through the parted waters, me and Mary trailing behind. "My Roseanna paid for what she did," she told him. "Your boy don't seem to be suffering any."

Chapter Twenty-Five

SEPTEMBER 1882

MY BROTHER CALVIN was out back shooting at a hawk that had been plaguing our chickens all week. Every once in a while we'd hear a shot and everybody in the kitchen would jump.

"Fanny, go tell your brother to stop that shooting," Alifair ordered. "You'd think he'd have more sense. Ma is spooked. And he should have more respect for his brothers."

Alifair was in a fine fettle, like she always was when things got bad in our house. Trouble brought out the best in her. And we had it now, all right. The kitchen was full of neighbor women who'd brought food, like you always do at funerals. Alifair had been in charge since two days ago when Jim came and told us that my brothers were dead.

All three of them—Tolbert, Pharmer, and Bud—shot by Devil Anse and his men under the pawpaw trees on the Kentucky side of the Tug, the day after we visited them at the Mate Creek Schoolhouse. After Devil Anse had promised Ma that he'd keep them alive. Shot in cold blood.

I saw their bodies when Jim and Calvin brought them home yesterday. I peeked into the parlor when Ro and Alifair and neighbor women were washing and dressing them.

They were full of bullet holes. I don't think I'll ever be able to go into our parlor again.

All I could think of was what Tolbert had said to Ma when Mary and I and baby Cora went with her into that schoolroom. The same thing Mary had said. "Don't beg for our lives, Ma. Don't ever beg a Hatfield. And don't ever believe what they tell you. Send for Pa."

Ma hadn't sent for Pa, who was still in Pikeville waiting for his boys to be delivered there by the sheriff's officers. She'd believed in the Lord setting places for my brothers in the midst of men armed with Spencer rifles. And now she was in the parlor with Tolbert's wife, Mary, little Cora, and Roseanna, saying, "I believed Devil Anse. I had his promise." Or allowing how God was going to welcome her boys into heaven. It was enough to make a person never want to pray again.

Today, the first day of September, was the funeral. Three fresh graves were dug high on a hill above the creekbed road. A secret place where they couldn't be found. I still couldn't believe my brothers were gone. Even though Yeller Thing had warned me.

Where did they go? To Ma's heaven? Would there be bees for Pharmer to tend there? Pheasants for Bud to hunt? What would Tolbert do on this first day of September, with the air cooling and the woods calling?

I worked my way around to the back of the house, past clusters of men in Sunday suits and hats, some with gold watch chains dangling right next to their pistols. Others jawing, with rifles poised in one hand. Neighbors and McCoys. I didn't even know who all some of the McCoys were. But they raised their hats and mumbled condolences as I passed.

I nodded politely, feeling very grown up. I was wearing a new brown calico and a white apron. At nine, men raised their hats to you in these mountains. At fifteen or sixteen a girl wed. There was my sister Trinvilla talking with Will Thompson, the preacher's son, who'd been coming around courting her regular-like this summer. And she was fourteen, but a true woman already. I went down to the chicken coop, where Calvin was sitting under a tree, waiting for that hawk. He nodded curtly to me. I sat down. "Alifair said to stop shooting. It's spooking Ma."

"Ma spooks herself," he said.

"Alifair says it isn't fitting now."

"It's fitting, long as that old hawk keeps at our chickens. He already got one this morning."

"She says you should have more respect for your brothers."

He patted his gun. He called it Trixie. "This is the only thing folks around here respect," he said solemnly. "And as far as Tolbert, Pharmer, and Bud go, wherever they are they want me to get that old chicken hawk, Fanny. Just like they want me to get those bloodsucking

Hatfields. And if Ma weren't so set on stopping Pa, we'd all be off hunting them properlike soon's the funeral is over. But she isn't goin' to let us. I heard them arguing about it last night."

I had, too. All night, it seemed, the low rumbling of Pa's voice and the high-pitched begging of Ma's had come through their bedroom door. This morning they'd scarce looked at each other.

"Pa blames her for the boys," Calvin said. "And so do I. She shouldn't of stopped Jim from sending for him and getting up a posse. She shouldn't of gone herself and made deals with old Devil Anse. She had no right. So it isn't my shooting that's spooking her this morning, Fanny. It's her own conscience. So go along now while'st I get myself this hawk."

I got up. "What'll I tell Alifair?"

"That as soon's this day is over, I'm gonna teach her to shoot a gun. And you, too. The day is coming soon when we may need you all to know. I'll be along directly. Go on, now. I need some more time alone here with Trixie and that old hawk."

I thought how he needed less time with Trixie. Less time with guns. Maybe they all did. But I didn't say it.

"There's something," I said, "and I don't know who to tell it to, now that Tolbert's gone."

He looked up and nodded sympathetically.

"Bill. He's upstairs in his room. And he's crying."

He blinked, but otherwise his face didn't change. "I know, Fanny," he said sadly. "He cried all last night. Says it was him who knifed Ellison and it's him who should be dead, and not Bud. We're gonna have a heap of grief with Bill, Fanny. You tell Alifair if she wants a worry, she's got one. Right upstairs."

"I tried to tell her about Bill this morning. She won't listen."

He sighed. "Well, why don't you try and talk to him then, Fanny? Seems to me you both need a friend about now."

I started back to the house. As I was halfway there I heard the shot, heard Calvin's shout of glee. "Good girl, Trixie. We got him."

In the kitchen I grabbed a cup of acorn Indian pudding and another of coffee. "Where you going with that?" Alifair asked.

"Bringing it to Bill. He's had no breakfast."

She held out her hands. "Anybody who doesn't come to the table doesn't get breakfast."

I stepped back, clutching my booty. "Bill needs it. He's upstairs crying," I said fiercely. "And I aim to bring it to him."

Several of the neighbor women had stopped what they were doing, stopped their chatter, and were watching. Alifair knew this. She sighed, held up her hands, and whirled around. "See what I have to put up with?" she said. Then to me. "Go on, but I want both of you down right quick. The funeral's soon starting."

I ran up the stairs, but I knew I hadn't bested her. I knew I'd pay for it later. And now there was no more Tolbert to rescue me from Alifair's clutches. Ma was so crazy with grief that if Alifair held my head under the pump and drowned me, Ma wouldn't discover it for three days. I stopped outside Bill's door and listened. No sound from inside. I pushed open the door and went in.

———

HE ATE. RIGHT where he was, on the floor by his bed. He was about starved. But he ate like a man who didn't know he was eating. Like he didn't even taste the food.

"My fault, Fanny," he said. "I should be dead, not Bud."

"It's nobody's fault," I told him.

He looked at me then for the first time. "Roseanna," he said. "Did you know? She brought that quilt home with her. She's got coffins for all of us on the edges. Just like she knew all the time they'd be shot. And she's just now moving Bud's, Pharmer's, and Tolbert's to the middle. Don't that beat all?"

I stared at him in horror.

"I want to die, Fanny. I told Roseanna. Know what she said? That she's felt that way for a long time. Then she said how a body can will themselves to die. Said she's seen it many a time when she was caring for sick folk. For no reason they just upped and died on her. Willed it. Well, that's what I aim to do then, I told her. You just better get my coffin moved to the middle."

"No," I told him.

"How can I live, Fanny, with Bud gone and it bein' my fault? No, I know what's best for old Bill. Come on now, don't you cry. You're so little and purty. You're the only sane McCoy. Come on now, let's go on down to the funeral. I'm gonna play my fiddle. 'Amazing Grace.' How you think that'll be on my fiddle?"

I clutched his hand as we went downstairs. "It'll be fine," I said. "It'll be just wonderful."

I was crying so I could scarce see and almost tripped going down. But Bill held on to me.

Chapter Twenty-Six

BILL PLAYED "Amazing Grace" at the funeral. And it was right fine.

Afterward, when people were eating all the food, I found Ro out in the yard near the herb garden.

"Poor little Fanny," she said. "Lost Tolbert. Your favorite brother."

"I heard you've got his coffin on your quilt. And Bud's and Pharmer's. Is Bill's there, too?"

"Hush." She set her plate down and reached out to grab and hug me. "Hush, don't let Pa and Ma hear you about the quilt."

I pulled away from her. "Pa said don't you ever put any McCoy names on it, Ro. Why'd you do it?"

"You still don't understand about that quilt now, baby, do you? It's more than just a quilt. It's a family history, like a Bible. I wanted it for my little Sarah Elizabeth."

"She's dead." I hadn't meant it to sound so cruel, so final, but I was angry.

"I know," she said softly. "And now somehow because she is gone to the angels I want to finish it proper-like. Because I started it for her."

Something inside me, deep inside, something that was part of my bones made me know she was lying. It frightened me. Because I was seeing Ro, my beloved sister, in a different light for the first time. *How could she have put our names on her quilt?* The thought of it ate into me, disturbed something I didn't want disturbed, brought it out of the woods and made me face it down, like I'd faced Yeller Thing.

My sister Ro was crazy. Crazy with grief over Sarah Elizabeth, teched in the head because Johnse had wed Nancy. Why hadn't anyone seen it? Because she'd been so good, nursing Alifair and all those others who'd come down sick?

"Did you tell Bill that a person can will himself to die?" I asked.

She nodded and sighed. "I've seen it, honey."

"But why did you have to tell Bill?"

"Why?" She gave that soft laugh of hers. And her voice! Oh, how it seeped into me, finding all my hurt places, just how it'd always done all my life. Her voice, so sweet, like dripping honey, had always made things all right with me. Had always put my fears to rest. Now that same voice was saying things I couldn't abide.

"Honey, I tried to help Bill. Because I know how he feels. Because I want to die, too. I just wanted to help him, is all."

"Stop it!" I stood up. "You're not going to die, Ro. And neither is Bill."

She smiled up at me. "Of course not, honey. No more dying. We've had enough of that, haven't we?" Her voice, putting my fears to rest, soothed me. But in her eyes there was a look I ran from, a look that warned me of what was to come. So I ran from her. Just like I ran from Yeller Thing.

———

"ISN'T YOUR BROTHER Calvin coming to school anymore, Fanny?"

It was a day in October struck through with enough color for one of Ma's quilts. The sky was a perfect blue. I looked up from gathering my things to take my leave. "It's hunting season, Mr. Cuzlin."

He smiled down at me. "Oh, I know that." He waved an arm around the schoolroom. "Even the seven-year-olds aren't here these days. You can hear the shots of the hunt from miles away. But Calvin hasn't been here once since school started this fall. Is he not coming back?"

"He's never said. But I heard him say there's nothing more you can teach him. He wishes there was."

"And Trinvilla?"

"She's to wed the reverend's son in December. She's making ready."

He nodded. "I'm sorry for all the trouble you folks have had. The Hatfields have been indicted here in Kentucky, you know. I've been following it in the newspapers."

I nodded. Ever since the killings, newspapers had been filled with stories. About murder under the paw-paw trees. About bloody killings. Pa wouldn't allow them in the house. We kept them away from Ma. "But the Hatfields are in West Virginia," I said.

I said no more. In our family you never spoke of troubles to anyone outside. I longed to tell Mr. Cuzlin, though, of how things were at home. How Bill had been tending the cows since Alifair's sickness and now Alifair made me do it, because Bill no longer did his chores. He wandered the woods. Not hunting, just wandering.

Because Pa was afraid to let us girls go to and from school on our own, Bill was supposed to escort us. He did mornings, but by afternoon he seldom came. I'd have lied to Alifair and told her he did, but Adelaide would run right home and snitch on Bill. Then he'd be in trouble. I'd have to go and fetch him home for supper. Most times I'd find him at my brothers' graves.

I wanted to tell Mr. Cuzlin how Pa and Ma argued all the time now about him wanting to lead raids into West Virginia to bring in the men who'd shot my brothers. How Pa kept organizing posses. The men would gather in our front yard, armed and ready. And then Ma would talk Pa out of it, and the men would have to go home.

I wanted to tell how rumor had it that Johnse had taken part in the killings of my brothers. No, I couldn't tell any of this. "I have to go," I said. "I have chores at home."

"Wait." He went across the room and fetched a book. *A Christmas Carol* by Charles Dickens. "Calvin will like it," he said.

I thanked him and went out into the October day. I wouldn't give the book to Calvin. But I couldn't tell Mr. Cuzlin that. Dickens was as far away from Calvin now as the man in the moon.

Adelaide ran on ahead. She was closer than ever to Alifair since the boys' deaths. But others in our family were shifting allegiances. Now that Trinvilla was to wed, Alifair had pushed her away. Calvin and Floyd had joined forces, both angry at Ma for keeping Pa from hunting Hatfields. Floyd, never one to fight, was ready to fight now. My only friend was Bill, even though he was only half there in his head.

We worried for him, wandering the woods, because Hatfields were crossing into Kentucky. Just last week my brother Sam and two of his friends were going to have a turn of corn ground at the mill at Dails Fork, when one of his friends was shot by Hatfields who'd crossed the Tug and come into our territory. That was as unheard of as black bears breaking into your larder.

When I got home from school, Alifair was waiting at the back door, wiping her hands on her apron. "Where's Bill? He didn't come fetch you all again?"

"You know already," I said. "Adelaide told you."

"Don't get fresh. Give me your things, then get to the barn and get the cows milked. They're waiting. Then go fetch Bill. I saw him at the graveyard. What's this?" She peered at the book.

"From Mr. Cuzlin. For Calvin."

She tossed the book away. It landed in the kitchen garden. "Dickens? Is that man crazy? You know where Calvin is? With Pa and Jim, invading West Virginia.

They brought back Tom Chambers today, one of the men who killed the boys. Does that sound like he needs Dickens?" She went into the house. I picked up the book and took it with me to the barn to milk the cows.

It was coming on to dark when I went up the hill above the creekbed road. I heard the music before I got to the top. Bill was playing his fiddle softly. The sun still cast a faint light in the west. He was backlit by the light, kneeling by the graves. I waited until he was finished playing.

"You gotta come home, Bill."

He looked at me. "Tolbert always liked 'How Great Thou Art.' "

I nodded. "Supper, Bill. Come on home. Please?"

He cradled his fiddle in his arms, looking around. "It's so purty up here."

I walked up the hill farther and reached out my hand to him. I didn't want him getting notions about how purty a grave was. "Come on, Bill, venison stew for supper."

He gave me his hand and we went down the hill together.

Chapter Twenty-Seven

WINTER 1883

YESTERDAY A FUNERAL and today a wedding. That's what I thought, watching Trinvilla stand in church beside Will Thompson while his father asked her, "Wilt thou take this man?"

Yesterday the same people, standing in church blowing on their hands for the cold in spite of warmth from the old pot stove, had stood stamping their feet at the cemetery at the mouth of Peter Creek while Reverend Thompson prayed over another McCoy, ambushed by Hatfields, a distant kin.

As Trinvilla answered yes, two men stood guard with long rifles outside the small church. Yesterday, McCoys were so armed at the cemetery it looked like they were expecting General Grant and his army. But with good reason.

While Reverend Thompson had prayed over the casket, "Vengeance is mine, sayeth the Lord," we could see Hatfields gathered all in a row on horses across the Tug. Pa expected them to fire their high-powered Winchester rifles across the water at us any minute.

After the funeral Reverend Thompson came over to Pa. "I'm a man of the Lord, Ranel. I have to stay out of this fight. If the Hatfields need me to bury any of their dead, I must do so."

"It's all right," Pa had said. "Just pray over our dead and marry our children."

It was two days into the new year when Trinvilla wed, cold as the inside of the Devil's ear. We tramped back to the house in the snow. And even though the men were all armed, there was a mood of merriment. Back at the house my brother Floyd broke out the rum. Bill, looking pale and thin, started his fiddle music. The parlor had been cleared of furniture for dancing. The kitchen was full of people and good smells. In the upstairs bedroom that Trinvilla shared with Adelaide and Alifair, I watched as Adelaide helped my sister pack her things.

"Baltimore!" Adelaide said. "What I'd give to see Baltimore!"

"It isn't as if we're staying at any fancy hotel," Trinvilla said. "We'll be guests at Will's aunt and uncle's home. But it is grand, I hear."

"But think! You wed. And going away with a man!" Adelaide was starry-eyed.

Trinvilla laughed. "I feel the fine lady in this dress Ma made. Do I look it?"

"You look finer than anybody. They'll love you in Baltimore," Adelaide told her. "There, you're all packed. I've got to go downstairs and help Alifair with the food."

Left alone with Trinvilla, I did not know what to say. I think she felt the same way. She sat down on her bed and smiled at me. "Adelaide won't marry," she said. "So you're next, Fanny."

I shook my head no. "I'm only eleven."

"Time to start making your Wedding-ring quilt. I had my eye on Will since I was ten."

She was just sixteen. "You're so grown up, Trinvilla," I said.

"How come you never call me Twinny, like the others?"

I blushed. "We were never close. You were always on the side of Alifair."

"I went along with her because I wasn't strong enough to say no. I saw how she treated you. I'm sorry for that, Fanny. But you stood up to her, always. I thought that was right fine."

My eyes widened. "You did?"

"Yes. Now listen. I'm going away. It's time to say some things. I don't know if we'll stay in Baltimore or if we'll come back here. But if we do, we'll move more inland. You know the governors of both states are telling people to move more inland, to get away from the fighting."

I nodded yes.

"Jim is thinking on it. And Calvin is trying to make

Ma and Pa move. But they won't hear of it. Ma told Calvin the only way they'll get her out of this house is to carry her out. They like it, Fanny, all the fighting. Do you know what first drew me to Will Thompson? He's like his pa. He wants no part of it. Around here you have to be either for the Hatfields or the McCoys. You have to choose sides. Well, Will and I are staying out of it. I'm tired of it, Fanny, all the killing. When you cast an eye on a boy, be sure he's out of it. And when you wed, get away. Stay out of it, Fanny, do. Or it'll destroy you."

I couldn't answer this outburst. Never did I expect it from quiet Trinvilla.

"I love Ma and Pa," she said, "but they're crazy. This whole family is. You know how Alifair acted with me when I got betrothed to Will? Like I betrayed her! Wouldn't help with my Wedding-ring quilt, wouldn't listen to me about my plans. Imagine! She expected me to not wed. To stay home and do her bidding. Well, she's got Adelaide as her indentured servant, but not me. I aim to make a life of my own. And not stay around here and wait for the next shooting and go to the next funeral and see Bill mourning at the grave and Calvin waiting to run out on the next raid. And Roseanna looking like she should be in the grave."

She stood up, smoothed her dress, and smiled. "Enough," she said. "If you ever get tired of it all, Fanny, you can come and live with us."

"Thank you," I said. Then I kissed her. "I wish you well, Trinvilla. I do."

She put her arm around me and we went downstairs.

Afterward I stood at the window as they drove off in the buggy to Will's father's for overnight. *I never even knew my sister*, I thought. *And now I've lost her.*

———

FOR A DAY or so I pondered what Trinvilla had said. I tried not to think of the feud. I didn't listen when Pa told how there was a five hundred thousand dollar price on Devil Anse's head. Or when Calvin told how he'd met two detectives in Pikeville who were set on capturing Hatfields. Or when Adelaide said how Nancy and Johnse had a baby boy. I tried to stay out of it.

I tried to think about school. I was doing well in my sums, geography, history, and English. I was getting so good at milking the cows that I could read while I did it. Just lay a book open on my lap. I read the book intended for Calvin and lost myself in Mr. Dickens's England at Christmas.

I told nobody about Roseanna's quilt having our names on it. Roseanna left us right after the wedding and went to stay with Tolbert's Mary, who was thinking of moving back to Louisville, where her parents lived.

Winter closed in around us, bringing some heavy storms, so that we had all we could do just to care for the animals, clear the yard, and get back and forth to school.

One night the first week in February, after it had snowed a fine needlelike snow all day, I came back into the house from milking the cows and Bill hadn't come home. It was nigh onto dark. Pa was tying a rope from the house to the barn to use for a guideline if more snow came. We had supper and nothing was said about Bill. After I'd helped Adelaide and Alifair clean up, I put some food in a pot, then started getting on my outside clothes.

"Where do you think you're going?" Alifair demanded.

"To take Bill some food. In case you haven't noticed, he hasn't come home."

"You take off that coat. If you didn't spoil him so by bringing food up there, he might come home. You're not going out to slip into the ravine and nobody'll know it. Besides, he's probably warm and cozy in a corncrib someplace. He's not stupid, even though he makes like he is."

But he wants to die, I thought. *You don't understand.*

Pa came in the door then, his hair and beard covered with ice. "Your sister's right," he said. "Bill can take care of himself. Leave him be." His tone brooked no argument.

"You're just doing it to be mean," I told Alifair.

That night I was the last one to blow out the oil lamp in the kitchen and go up to bed. I waited and waited for Bill, torn between wanting to put on my coat and go fetch him and fear of what Pa would do if I went out and got lost in the snow.

Bill, I thought, *Bill, why don't you come home? Are you safe in a corncrib somewhere? Why wouldn't you ever take a gun with you like Pa and Calvin said, so you don't get ambushed?*

I went to bed. Under my quilts I listened to the howling wind, to the needlelike snow against the window. Once I thought I heard something outside and got up to look out.

There it was. Eyes glowing, yellow-green. Moving through the snow like it was summer wheat. I sat up half the night trembling and finally went to sleep. At dawn the sun shone, sparkling on tree limbs and fence posts. After I milked the cows, I walked to Floyd's. He came with me up the hill to the cemetery. From halfway there I saw the vultures in the naked trees overhead. Crows called. Everything echoed. Floyd told me to stay back, he'd go up. But I said no, I was coming, too.

And there, at the graves, we found Bill. Frozen stiff with his fiddle in his hands. His eyelashes were crusted with snow, his face bluish white. Floyd had to carry me down the hill, I was so crazy with grief, then go back up with Calvin and a sled to fetch Bill down.

Chapter Twenty-Eight

SPRING 1886

"WHAT ARE YOU doing here, Fanny McCoy? Don't you go to school anymore?"

I turned from the long white pine counter at the Pikeville General Store. Nancy McCoy. A baby in her arms and a knee-high at her skirts. "Hello, Nancy. Yes, I still go. But Ma's sending me to stay the night with Martha."

"Oh, that's right. Your brother Jim moved his family to Saylorsville. Considerable smart of him. Keep his family safe." Her mouth quivered.

I set down the goods I'd bought—some crackers, tallow candles, and coffee beans—and walked over to her. "You have a new baby."

"Yes. This is Stella. She's four months old. Isn't she darlin'?"

I took the baby up and admired it. But I was seeing Nancy. She was older, and it was downright eerie. Some of the old Nancy was still there in the face, but just when you glimpsed it, it was gone. The new Nancy was still pretty, but now there were lines around the mouth. And something shadowy in the eyes. "How is Johnse?" I handed the baby back.

The mouth quivered again. "I'm a-leavin' him. Why else would I be in Kentucky?" The beautiful violet eyes brimmed with tears, and she hugged her baby close.

"What happened, Nancy?"

"What didn't happen? He's been drinkin'. When he's in his cups those Hatfields can get him to do anything. His people beat up my sister Mary and her mother-in-law, Mrs. Daniels, in a masked raid. Left 'em bleedin' and unconscious. Johnse's brother Cap was at the head of that. Mary's husband said so. I told Johnse I won't stay with him if his family hurts my family anymore. He promised they wouldn't. Then they went and killed my brother Jeff."

We'd heard about all that, of course. It was the reason Pa and my brothers Jim and Sam were off on a raid now into West Virginia, because of Jeff McCoy's death last week. It's why I was going to stay with Martha. Because Jim would be away. Ro would be there, of course. That was another reason I was going.

In the last two years I'd seen my sister Ro maybe four times. We'd had a fight after Bill died. I blamed her for telling him a body could will themselves to die. Ma didn't know the reason for our fussing. But she'd finally said enough. "There's feuding going on outside this family. We don't need to add to it."

"And then last night Johnse came in drunk and pointed a gun at me," Nancy was saying. "I told him no more. It isn't bad enough his brother Cap shot my brother Jeff." Her voice trailed off, then picked up again. "I'm sorry about your brother Bill dyin' and all. I haven't seen ye since."

Bill. Gone over two years now, but the pain inside was new every time somebody said his name. I blamed myself for Bill. I should have gone out that night and brought him home. Over and over again in my head the last two years I'd asked myself why I hadn't. Why hadn't I gone against my family and been strong? Why hadn't I been strong enough, like Trinvilla?

"I have to go, Nancy." I picked up my old straw suitcase and my sack of goods. "Martha and Ro will be along any minute to fetch me in the buggy." I wanted to get outside and away from her. I didn't want her following, to give her howdy to Ro. I was on the outs with Ro, sure, but even I couldn't be the one to bring about a meeting between her and the woman who'd stolen away Johnse. Even though it looked like Ro was well shut of him.

———

MARTHA HAD A loom in the parlor. She said it was her great-grandmother's and was over a hundred years old. "It's a four-harness loom," she told us. " 'Bout a year ago I got Jim to get it out of the barn and set it up for me. Here, I'm making this bedcover."

We'd put the children to bed in the loft. Martha put

up coffee. Until now the little girls had kept us from talking of ourselves. Martha knew that Ro and I had been fussing. She knew this visit was a strain to me. But with her round, smiling face and sunny disposition, it was impossible to speak of trouble in front of Martha. She just wouldn't hold with it.

The bedcover was red and white. The wild-rose pattern. "It's beautiful," I said.

"Don't you like quilts?" Ro asked.

" 'Course I do," Martha said. "But my grandmother Gertrude taught me to weave like this, and I'm making this to hand down to my daughters. An heirloom. I just love heirlooms."

"I wanted my quilt for my Sarah Elizabeth," Ro said real sadlike. "But now I don't know who I'll give it to. Fanny, most likely."

"I don't want it," I told her.

Martha's innocent blue eyes went wide. "Why, Fanny McCoy, what an awful thing to say. You should be honored to have your sister's quilt."

I stared hard at Ro. It was clear that Martha knew nothing of the Coffin quilt. "I don't want it," I said again. I couldn't forgive Ro for putting Bill's coffin on the quilt.

Martha put a hand on my arm. "Honey, I know you two have been fussing. But don't let your dear mama hear you say that. It's cast her spirit down something awful. And don't ever say such in front of your brother Jim. Family's like religion to him. Why Ro is putting love into every stitch of that quilt of hers, I wager. Just like I'm putting love into every thread of my coverlet."

Love? I wanted to laugh. They stood, both of them, firm and set against me. *How unfair of Ro,* I thought. *How dishonest.* I loved Martha. I couldn't abide having her think ill of me. But she would now. And I couldn't explain. "I think I'll go to bed," I said.

"Maybe you'd best," Martha said coldly. "And think and pray on what you just said. This family needs to stick together. More now than ever before."

―――――

THERE WAS A three-quarter moon and its light came through the window of my small room. And I thought, *That's what woke me.* I'd been dreaming of Bill, dreaming that I was putting my coat on and going out the door to fetch him home. But when I went out the door there was a posse waiting there in our yard, armed and talking softly.

I sat up in bed. Why didn't those men stop talking? Didn't they know I was awake now? The night outside was bright as daylight. I peered out the window and gasped. Can you conjure people from dreams? A group of men sat in the front yard, exactly like in my dream, armed and talking softly, like it was broad daylight. They aimed to attack us!

I ran down the hall to wake Martha and Ro. In an instant they were up and looking out the window with me. "They aim to attack," I said. "They know Jim's away. Like they attacked Mary McCoy and Mrs. Daniels."

"Not while I've got any breath in me," Ro said. And

she turned and ran downstairs. We followed. In the kitchen she took up a long rifle from next to the fireplace.

"What will you do?" Martha stood there, wringing her hands.

"I can shoot," Ro said. "It's the one good thing Johnse Hatfield taught me." She unbolted the door and stepped out on the porch, the rifle set under her arm. "Can I help you, gentlemen?"

They stopped talking. There were at least six of them. Masked. Martha and I cowered just inside. These men could kill us all if they took the notion. Or beat us and make us cripples like Mrs. Daniels. Beside me I felt Martha trembling.

One of them urged his horse forward and spoke. "That you, Roseanna McCoy?"

"It's me. The fallen woman of Pike County."

Soft laughter. "We got no quarrel with you. Just come to warn Mrs. McCoy there. She better tell her husband to leave off huntin' Hatfields."

Ro had the gun aimed right at him. "She heard you. Now get off her land. And take your low-down women-beatin' men with you."

"That's right unkind, Roseanna. We don't beat up women."

"Tell that to Mary McCoy and her mother-in-law. Now git. Johnse taught me to use this."

Unbelievably, they went. Turned, pretty as you please, and rode off. Ro set down the gun and leaned against the doorjamb. Martha hugged her. "I'm so proud of you. You're so brave."

I looked at my sister Roseanna. And what I saw was not relief in her face. But disappointment. *She was sorry they didn't attack*, I thought. *She still wants to die.*

The thought struck me full-face. I wanted to throw up. Without another word I left the two women standing there, talking and consoling, and ran upstairs to bed.

Chapter Twenty-Nine

SPRING 1887

I WAS FOURTEEN, the oldest in the class. At fourteen most girls left school, but nobody said anything so I kept going. I helped Mr. Cuzlin with the little kids. He said I was right smart, that I should think about going to normal school and become a teacher.

"You'd have to go to Wirt County in West Virginia to school," he said. "They're turning out good teachers there and many will be teaching here in Kentucky."

I thanked him for his interest. "But I can't go to school in West Virginia," I said.

"If you pass the exam, you won't have to worry about tuition. I'll see to it that you don't."

"It isn't that." I looked at him. "No McCoy goes into West Virginia. They'd be shot dead in their tracks. Just yesterday my brother Jim and a deputy were caught there hunting Hatfields. Old Devil Anse made them kneel. Said they were going to die. The other deputy knelt, but not Jim. He opened his shirt and said, 'Shoot. I'd just as lief die standing on my feet.' "

"But he wasn't shot, was he?" Mr. Cuzlin said.

"No sir. Because Devil Anse said he was too brave. I'm not brave. They'd shoot me."

He looked so sad then. "Well," he said. "Maybe when this trouble is over. Think on it."

If he'd said I should go to Paris, France, it couldn't have been stranger to me. "I can't conjure up a life away from my family, Mr. Cuzlin. Besides, I'm Ma's mainstay. Alifair is gone most of the time on her healing missions. Adelaide's working with Aunt Cory to become a granny woman. Ma faints a lot. She needs me."

He said something funny then. "Fanny," he said, "sometimes we don't have to leave in order to get away. Sometimes all we have to do is choose."

Chapter Thirty

DECEMBER 31, 1887

I WAS FOURTEEN and it was the last day of the year. I worked alone in the kitchen making a supper for the occasion. Brunswick stew simmered on the stove. I was frying up a heap of potatoes. I'd made light bread and carrot pudding for dessert. Pa had been gone all day, but that was nothing new. It seemed of late that I didn't have a pa at all. He was either gone on raids into West Virginia or stone silent when he was home. Same with Calvin. We'd been lucky to get the hogs slaughtered this year.

Pa and Calvin had been all day in Pikeville. Ma was most of the day in her room. As if her fainting fits weren't enough, she now had influenza. Last time I checked her she was praying that Adelaide and Alifair would get home without being ambushed.

In December Pa and my brothers and a new deputy sheriff, name of Frank Phillips, had brought in Wall Hatfield, Devil Anse's brother. The whole month had been taken up with a trial. We just about had Christmas. Wall was sentenced to life in prison for his part in my brothers' killings. But everybody said it was illegal. 'Cause he'd been kidnapped from West Virginny. And while they were arguing should there be a new trial, Wall Hatfield up and died in prison.

Pa and Calvin had left to meet with men in Pikeville at first light. Before he'd left, Pa had told me to keep the doors locked. He was afraid of reprisals. Lord, I didn't have time to think of reprisals. I raced around like a chicken chased by a fox all day, caring for Ma, cooking, milking the cows, feeding the dogs, pigs, chickens, and horses.

It had commenced to snow about two in the afternoon and when I was bringing the milk cans in, I was looking down, for the snow was in my eyes. Then, halfway between the barn and the house, I heard it. The hissing. The growl. I stopped dead in my tracks and looked up.

There, by the corncrib, was Yeller Thing. Standing still, so's I got a look at him for the first time. Seemed like a cross between a wolf and a painter cat. Looked about starved, too. His head hung low and his eyes glowed at me. His tongue hung out about a foot long. 'Peared pure worn down like he needed a tonic. I knew it was Yeller Thing, for the stink of him. For a full minute we just stared at each other through the snow. "What you want with me?" I asked.

He only growled.

"You go 'way. You vamoose!" I don't know what made me brave. I was worn down myself from working, my hands were freezing, and now I had to worry about Adelaide and Alifair getting home safe, too. "That what you come to tell me? Well, my sisters will be right fine. You'll see!"

I went on with my milk cans. Mangy old dog is what he was. I wasn't a child anymore to be afeared of him.

Just about then, Adelaide drove in. She went about in a little cart that Floyd had made her. "Stopped by Mr. Chasen's to treat his arthritis," she said. "He allowed how he thought the Hatfields would be on the warpath on account of Wall dying."

"We didn't kill him," I reminded her.

"He said he heard they're tired of hiding in the mountains. That they've had to sell off land to buy food 'cause they couldn't farm. And to pay for men, guns, and lawyers."

We stamped the snow off our feet. "Can't we talk about something else?"

"Did you remember to give Ma her medicine?"

"Yes." She insisted that Ma have her "blood purifier." She mixed a spoonful of sulfur in a pint of honey. "She took it, but I still think we should call Dr. Grey."

"She'll be better soon. No need for Dr. Grey."

I slammed the lid down on the Brunswick stew. "Tomorrow, I'm fetching him!"

"Heavens! Fetch him. Do. You'll see I'm right." She tossed her head and ran upstairs.

Pa and Calvin came in next, worn down and freezing. I fetched Pa's slippers, got Calvin some rum. Then came Alifair. I breathed a sigh of relief. My family was home, safe. *You see, Yeller Thing,* I thought as Ma said the prayer, *your day is over. My sisters are home and safe.*

———

FUNNY HOW THINGS come back to you. I remember how careful I was to store those leftovers after supper, how I cleaned up the kitchen. Ma went to bed directly after supper. Alifair and Adelaide went upstairs to confer. Calvin read a newspaper. He was twenty-four, tall and lanky. I thought about offering him one of the new books Mr. Cuzlin had given me. Another Dickens novel. But then he took up his Trixie and commenced to clean it. I waited for him to speak to me. When he didn't I said good night and went to my own room to read.

———

THEY'VE ASKED ME about it since. So many people. What did you first hear? Was it late? Were you the first awake?

It's all a jumble to me—noise, shrieks, crashing glass. I only know we went to bed in a warm darkened house. My supper had been good. Everybody said so. My family was home safe, so there was no sense in even thinking of Yeller Thing. An old mangy dog is all he was, all he'd ever been. Too many stories of haints in these parts was the trouble. My last thought was to fetch Dr. Grey tomorrow for Ma. Pa was worried about her. I'd ride myself and fetch him after Adelaide left.

No sooner had I closed my eyes, it seemed, than the sickening sound of crashing glass woke me. Then there was the crack of a gunshot and the thud as it hit the pine-log walls of the house. My first thought was that something had exploded downstairs. Had I left the Brunswick stew on the stove? Once my feet were on freezing floors, I knew it was not the Brunswick stew. I'd put that away. Then I heard Calvin's racing feet in the hall, his cry.

"Hatfields, Pa! They're attackin'!"

Everybody was running then. My sisters raced downstairs in flannel nightgowns, and I followed. Pa was buttoning his shirt and grabbing a gun. Against the white snow outside, the jagged glass of the kitchen window was outlined. Frigid air came in.

Calvin was fastening on his gunbelt. "Out by the corncrib. 'Pears to be a bunch of 'em."

I stood stock-still. *The corncrib!* Yeller Thing! He *was* real! Again, he'd come to warn me!

"Put your mother back to bed," Pa ordered me.

There was Ma, leaning on a chair in the kitchen, looking like a scarecrow. Adelaide started leading her upstairs when Calvin ran to kiss her. "Don't worry none, Ma. They won't get in. They'll have to kill me first." Then he looked at Pa. "Up to the loft, Pa. That's where we have the advantage. You girls, stay away from the windows."

"Come on out, Ranel!" The voice boomed outside. Jim Vance. "Come on out and surrender, if you want to save your family."

Pa? Surrender? I guess that's when I knew it was over. He'd die first. We all would. That's when I knew we were finished.

Chapter Thirty-One

DECEMBER 31, 1887

IT WENT ON for what seemed like hours, the shouts of the men outside, the gunfire, the scrambling inside, the footsteps and shouts of Pa and Calvin upstairs.

"Come on out, Ranel," the voices kept demanding. "Come on out. We want you. We're sick and tired of your comin' into West Virginia and makin' us hide away from our homes and womenfolk. We aim to make you pay for Wall dyin' in prison. We want this over, now!"

Adelaide cried. She clung to me in the kitchen, where we hunkered low by the old cast-iron stove, and cried and trembled like a baby. "They aim to kill us, Fanny."

I held on to her. "They won't. Pa and Calvin won't let 'em."

"If only we had more men."

"I should get my coat on and run for Floyd," I said. I was sure I could sneak out. But every time I made a move to leave her, Adelaide clung to me. "Don't go! Don't leave me!"

So I stayed. To hear bullets thudding into the house walls. To hear the shouts and cusses and threats from the men outside, the braying and barking of our dogs, Adelaide's wailing, Calvin's voice upstairs, every once in a while Pa's. To shiver in my nightdress next to Adelaide, even though we were beside the stove.

"Maybe we should go upstairs with Ma and Alifair," Adelaide said.

I thought that a good idea. But just as we were pondering it, the light in the kitchen changed. A yellow glow cast on the walls from outside. Adelaide raised her head to see and gasped. "They've got pine-knot torches."

"We're a-goin' to set the house afire, Ranel," came a shout, "lessin' you come out now!"

The only answer was a volley of shot from the upstairs windows. Each time the guns fired I jumped. The sound was so sickening. It echoed in the cold air.

Next thing we heard was a terrible scream. "I been hit! I been hit!" we heard from outside.

"That's it, Ranel!" And with that, another kitchen window smashed on the front wall, and a flaming bunch of faggots made crackling brightness where no brightness should be, in the middle of the kitchen floor. At once the bundle of twigs flared orange, eating, devouring. Then came another, and another, and another followed, making a circle of flame and smoke that filled my eyes and brain, destroying the herbs hanging from the rafters, Ma's calico curtains, making new curtains of thick, sour smoke.

I had to get us out. "Come on," I said, "upstairs, Adelaide." I had to drag her. We bumped into Calvin and Pa, scrambling down. "The kitchen's on fire." I choked out the words.

"Alifair, c'mon down here and get to the buckets," Calvin yelled. We kept buckets of water in the house just in case of fire. Maybe three. At the most four. The flames in the kitchen were growing, hissing, growling like some live beast. I stood there, staring, thinking, *Now we won't have the Brunswick stew to eat anymore, and it was so good.* Then somebody pushed me aside.

"Alifair!" I heard Calvin yell again. Then I saw Alifair go right through the smoke, grab up the buckets, and start thowing the water on the flames. The puncheon floor was warm, smoldering, under my bare feet. Flames lapped at the beamed ceiling, feeding on everything in sight. The heat was near suffocating.

Calvin and Pa were firing out the kitchen windows. Pa's shirt was smoldering in back. Alifair threw some water on it. "We need more water, Calvin," she yelled. "It's all give out."

I saw Calvin turn from the window, waving his arms like some haint in the smoke. One arm held Trixie.

"We gotta have more, Calvin," Alifair said, "or we'll be burned out. We'll be forced out, and they'll kill us all!"

"Can you sneak out to the well and get some?" They were standing not three feet from each other, but yelling through the smoke, because Pa was firing out and the men outside were firing in. Alifair already had her coat on over her nightgown. Smoke and flames were coming up through the floorboards now.

"By God," Calvin yelled. "They've put more torches under the house!"

"I'm goin' out now," Alifair said. She grabbed up a bucket.

"They'll shoot you," Pa yelled. I thought he hadn't been listening, but he had.

"It's either that or they shoot us all," Alifair told him. "Anyways, even they aren't low-down enough to shoot a woman fetching water to save her house!" And then she was gone, through the smoke, out the back door, and into the yard.

"Alifair!" Adelaide screamed, and tried to follow her. "Don't go, please!"

"Grab your sister," Pa yelled, "and shut her up! Get outa this room and see to Ma."

I took a-hold of Adelaide, who was screaming like a painter cat. I dragged her out of the kitchen. There was a sight of smoke in it now. I didn't know how Pa and Calvin were able to breathe, excepting that they were firing out of open windows. Every once in a while one of the shots from outside the house would thud against the walls. The sounds were soft thuds but horrible. Under my bare feet I felt broken glass. I tripped over something wooden, near fell, and righted myself. The world seemed to be gone howling mad all around me.

Then of a sudden the fearsome noise outside

stopped. A man's voice yelled, "Halt there! Who goes? Ranel? Have ye come out? Stop firing, boys."

And Alifair's voice in return. "It's me, Alifair. Is that you, Cap Hatfield?"

"It's me."

"Well, I come out for some water because my kitchen is burning. *My kitchen,* Cap Hatfield. And to me it's sacred. In all this fracas, did we ever come and burn your kitchen?"

I couldn't hear his reply. Adelaide was blubbering in my ear. "Hush!" I shook her.

"If you don't go back inna house, Alifair, I'm a-goin' to have to shoot you," came the voice that had allowed he was Cap.

"You? Shoot me?" And Alifair laughed. "We went to school together, Cap. I know you're big and bad now, but not big and bad enough to shoot a woman, are ye?"

Silence, except for the crackling of flames where the fire hadn't yet been dampened. Terrible silence. Then a shot, ringing and certain in the cold. Then Alifair's voice, strong no more, but begging. "Dear God. Sweet Jesus." Growing weaker and weaker, then nothing.

Adelaide broke loose from me and made for the door. Calvin yelled, "Damned varmints! They shot Alifair!" Pa yelled and made for the door then, too, but Calvin held him back. "She's on the ground, Pa. She ain't movin'. She's dead. Go out there, and you're next. I need you in here, Pa. Or they'll kill us all!"

"Hold on to your sister!" Pa shoved Adelaide at me. He looked like some demented god as he turned again to the window and recommenced firing. Then Adelaide broke from me and ran to the hall and stood screaming, "Ma, Ma! They shot Alifair!"

But Ma was already coming down the steps, her long hair around her shoulders, her boney hands groping the walls. "My Alifair? They shot her? Let me through!"

Nobody could stop her. When Pa tried, she seized up a piece of broken glass and threatened him with it. And with Isaiah. "And I stay at my post through all the watches of the night!" Then she went out into the night.

"Cover her," Calvin told Pa.

I could see Ma leaning over Adelaide and glaring up at a masked somebody who stood over her. His eyes reflected the firelight, glowed like Yeller Thing. "Get back inside, old hag."

Ma stood up and raised her fist. "I will encamp like David amongst you. I will encircle you with outposts and set up siege works against you. Prostrate you shall speak from the earth!"

I recollect thinking how right brave Ma was. And how I could never be.

Then the man raised his gun and swung it back, and I yelled, "No, no!" I lunged, and then it was Adelaide holding me back as the gun cut the cold night air and hit Ma, again and again.

Calvin charged out the door next into the yawning dark and raced to the corncrib, making it there somehow, then raised Trixie to take aim and was cut down by a ringing shot.

"No, no!" I was yelling it then, and Adelaide was holding me. Pa was bellowing for Adelaide to take me into the woods, to go out the back window. I stumbled along after Adelaide, followed her out the window like I was in a dream, feeling colder and stiller than Ma and Calvin and Alifair, colder and stiller than the freezing night air that filled up my lungs, then seeped forever into my heart.

Chapter Thirty-Two

JANUARY 1888

ME AND ADELAIDE made for the woods. In the midnight cold, bare of feet, we found our way, huddling and shivering together, to my old playhouse, where I found a tattered quilt to wrap us in. From there we could see our house burning, flames reaching into the night sky, smoke billowing. And against the firelit night, men dashing about, staining the earth with their shadows.

We waited, shivered, sobbed, and prayed while night owls hooted and all around us the stark trees shielded us as their own, though I'm sure they didn't want us as their own, tainted as we were. I'm sure they'd just as lief we left the quiet solitude they offered and went back into the howling world of madness as we had made it to be.

———

BY FIRST LIGHT the men were gone. Our house was a charred ruin with only the chimney still standing like a question mark against the lead sky. Pa came out of the hog pen, where he'd stayed the night, and ran for Floyd, who sent for Jim and Sam. They took Calvin and Alifair and covered them decentlike against the prying eyes of others who came to see. They took Ma up in a wagon. She was more dead than alive and with no sense about her whatsoever, which was a blessing of the Lord. Then they found me and Adelaide and carried us in blankets to a home that no longer was. Then we went with Ma to the Cline house, where Roseanna waited.

They said I kept babbling about how I had to go into the house and get the leftover Brunswick stew or we'd starve. I don't recollect that. I haven't made Brunswick stew since. Likely I'll never make it again.

———

WHEN THEY LAID Calvin and Alifair to rest in graves next to Pharmer, Tolbert, Bud, and Bill, I wasn't there. I was in Aunt Martha Cline's house, petting her cat and sitting in a corner with a comforter around me. Shadows and voices came and went all around me. When a loud noise happened, I jumped.

They say I was off my feed for a week. That I wouldn't let Roseanna near me, that Aunt Martha had to spoon broth into my mouth. That Dr. Grey had come and gone, and said I might never talk again. Or I might speak in tongues at supper. He couldn't rightly say.

I didn't speak in tongues at supper, but after about a week I started talking to the cat. They let me be. I knew that Ma was upstairs in a room, pure give out, and might be she wouldn't live. Reverend Thompson came.

Trinvilla and Will came. Pa came. Even Mr. Cuzlin came with books for me. I seized on the books and started reading. About other worlds and other peoples who had terrible heartache, who sweated blood for their dreams and cried in pain for their loves, and whose lives were all better than mine.

Adelaide wasn't with us. She went right to Aunt Cory's to stay. To go on with her granny work like nothing had happened. They say it was her way of not speaking, or talking only to a cat, or losing herself in books. They say when I started to speak again I said I had to do the chores. I kept wandering out in the cold to milk Aunt Martha's cows. That when they tried to stop me, I cried and allowed how Alifair would hold my head under the pump if I didn't get those cows milked right quick.

I recollect none of it at all.

All the newspapers said the attack on our house was the worst yet in the history of Kentucky. That not even the Indians who had once lived here and slaughtered settlers had done as bad as was done to us.

I do own that I recollect two things that happened in that time.

Pa came to Aunt Martha's and told Roseanna, who was nursing Ma, that it was all her fault. He didn't hold forth. He said it real quietlike. But I heard. "If'n you hadn't run off with Johnse," he told her, "none of it would've happened."

And I mind that once Ro came to where I was sitting with the cat in my lap and knelt on the floor in front of me. "I'm so sorry, Fanny," she said. "Oh, I'm so sorry."

I was talking by then, though not much. I petted the cat's head and looked at my sister. "Well now," I said, "you can just go and put Alifair's and Calvin's coffins in the middle of that quilt of yourn, can't you?"

She didn't know what all to say to that, of course. She just put her head down and sobbed. Then she stopped and looked at me again. "Isn't there anything I can do to make you forgive me?" she asked.

Until that minute I couldn't think of a thing. But then I did. "There is something."

"Yes, baby, anything."

"I'd admire for you to leave me alone." Never did I reckon I would say such. Never did I mean it so much, either.

Chapter Thirty-Three

SPRING 1888

I CAME BACK to being myself, of course. Or whatever of myself I could still find. I had to. Our family didn't hold with self-pity, everybody had their duties and was expected to do their best soon's they felt middling well. I helped Aunt Martha a bit around the house. I visited with Ma. Pa was away most all the time with posses he formed. The county judge himself, Mr. Tobias Wagnor, went to Frankfort to get arms for Pa and his men. I don't know where they kept them, but not in our new house in Pikeville that we moved into that spring. Ma wouldn't countenance it, she said.

"No guns in this house. I won't have it, Ranel. If'n I ever see a Winchester or even a Colt pistol, I'll get a smotherin' fit, for sure."

Ma got smothering fits all the time now.

While we were at Aunt Martha Cline's, Ro nursed Ma. I know it to be true that it was only Ro's nursing that brought Ma around again. You have to give the Devil his due.

Come right down to it, it wasn't nary a one of Adelaide's remedies, though she tried half a dozen. Not even Alifair's faith-healing group, who came one day and prayed over Ma and anointed her with oil. And acted like they expected her to get up and start dancing to fiddle music at supper. She didn't. And they went away disappointed, leaving Ma in tears with only Ro to comfort her, because at that time I was still talking only to the cat.

But my sister Ro brought Ma back with her care and soft words. Seems like she never left Ma's side in the month after the attack. By spring Ma was able to get off her couch and wobble around with a cane a little. But she was all crooked, like a bent tree. She couldn't hold her head straight. Had to turn her whole body to look you in the face. But she still praised Jesus every chance she got.

In April we moved into the Pikeville house and Ro came along with us. Nobody asked her and nobody told her she couldn't. We just all knew Ma couldn't do without her. So she came. But we still didn't talk much, me and Ro. We exchanged sentences is what we did.

"Did Ma eat any of her supper?" she'd ask.

I'd answer no. Then she'd ask when Pa was expected home. Or would I go to the store for her. And I'd answer. But we didn't speak to each other, only at each other. I guess we both just knew there was nothing more to say.

All that summer Pa, his men, and my brothers raided

West Virginia and brought back men who'd attacked our house that night. On one of these trips they brought in Ellison Mounts.

———

I HATED THE house in Pikeville from the minute we moved in. It was a small dwelling, not like our place on Blackberry Creek. The only good part was the river out back. I'd go down there of a summer afternoon, read, and watch fishermen go by in small boats. They came regular-like and after a while would wave at me. I'd wave back. There was one man who wore a wool hat, even in the middle of summer. Another brought his small grandson along. Still another had his small black dog in the boat with him. I'd conjure up lives for them, families, homes.

Someone said that creek found its way to West Virginny. I worried some that Hatfields would learn where we lived now and come by boat to attack us. But it didn't happen, and so I stopped worrying. In September I wanted to go back to school, but it was too far so Mr. Cuzlin came once a week to tutor me. He wouldn't take any money for it, either. All he wanted, he said, was for me to study, serious-like, on the idea of going to normal school and becoming a teacher.

I looked forward to his visits more than I like to lay claim to. But I couldn't bring my mind around to thinking on becoming a teacher. In my head there was no future for any of us at all.

Chapter Thirty-Four

FALL 1889

THE REASON I know that Ellison Mounts didn't kill my sister Alifair is more than because I heard Cap Hatfield talking with her that night just afore she was shot. It's because Reverend Thompson told me.

It was September. Pa was on another raid. Aunt Martha Cline had come to the little house in Pikeville to visit Ma, like she did every so often. I was in the parlor, studying. My sister Ro was upstairs in bed. She'd been sickly for the last month and nobody knew what ailed her. But while the bright blue skies of fall and the flaming colors beckoned outside, inside Ro roamed the house in her nightdress, not talking, not eating, just telling us all to leave her be, and getting thinner and thinner. Adelaide, who came home once a month like our sheep used to do, had doused her with remedies a week ago. Nothing helped.

I'd finished packing. I was going to Saylorsville to

visit Trinvilla and Will. They'd built a new house there last summer. It was Aunt Martha's idea that I go. I needed to get out of the house, she said. She and Ma were in the kitchen talking.

"I just can't stop Ranel," Ma was saying. "His mind is set on all this killing."

"Then don't stop him," Aunt Martha Cline said. "He's got no more homeplace, no more crops. He's got only his kin to revenge. It's proper for him to bring the Hatfields to justice, Sarah."

"How can it be proper to kill?"

Aunt Martha Cline's voice rose. "You preached prayer instead of action to your husband for so long, Sarah! You'd still have all your children if you hadn't. And now you've got Roseanna failing."

"Roseanna's grieving 'cause she heard Nancy is to wed Frank Phillips. She's grieving for that scoundrel Johnse," Ma said. "All she needs is a tonic."

Aunt Martha made a scoffing sound. "You live in your own world, Sarah. You always did."

———

I SUPPOSE REVEREND Thompson was kin to me, being father-in-law to my sister. I just couldn't think of a reverend as kin. I had trouble sitting at table with him, watching him eat and talk of everyday things. But it never bothered Trinvilla at all. It was part and parcel of how she'd changed since that day of her wedding, I suppose. She was a full woman at twenty-one, with notions from living in Baltimore, with her own house spread around her, a baby in a cradle, and a lawyer husband. She headed up committees in her father-in-law's church. I'd lost her again before I'd found her. Snobbish, she was. It was the only word I could put to how she acted. Confused as I was, I had to find meaning where I could.

"How's Roseanna?" Reverend Thompson asked when there was a lull in conversation.

"Middling," I answered. "Ma can't put a finger on what's ailing her."

He smiled. "I spoke to Johnse just yesterday."

I gaped, waiting. Something was coming, I was sure of it.

"I minister to folk on both sides of the river, Fanny. You must remember that. I take pride that both Hatfields and McCoys trust me. I like to think I've quenched some fires on both sides and kindled some understanding."

"Yes sir." He was rooting around it like a hound dog. All that talk of quenching and kindling fires. I looked at my sister. Under the soft light of the kerosene lamps, she glowed. Whatever he was getting at she knew about it. *Imagine,* I thought. *Being privy to what a reverend was thinking!*

"Johnse is worried about Roseanna," he said. "He heard she was took sick. And he asked after your ma, too."

I bridled. "He's got more nerve than a Yankee at a Southern camp meeting," I said. "After they raided our house that night."

"Now, now, Fanny," the reverend said soothingly. "Johnse wasn't there that night. I can vouch for that.

You think he'd be part of that killing and maiming? He still loves Roseanna."

Before I could give my opinion on that bit of hogwash, he went on.

"Jim Vance attacked your ma. Johnse's brother Cap shot Alifair."

"Then why have they got Ellison Mounts in prison for it?"

"Because," he answered softly, "Cap promised Mounts five hundred dollars, a rifle, and a saddle, if he'd take the blame. Promised he'd spring him from jail before they hanged him."

I stared at the man in disbelief. Then at my sister and Will. Trinvilla smiled in a way that made me want to smack her the way I did when she tattled on me to Alifair. "It's true," she said.

"What's it all got to do with me?" I asked.

"In the spirit of Godly forgiveness and forbearance that I myself preach and your sister and brother-in-law practice in this home," the reverend said, "I have a letter to Ro from Johnse. I'd like for you to deliver it to her."

I felt a blinding light behind my eyes. My head hurt. My food turned to sawdust in my mouth. "Aunt Martha Cline was just this day telling Ma how foolish she was with all her forgiveness and praying," I said. "And how, if she'd let Pa go after the Hatfields sooner, my brothers and Alifair might still be alive."

Nobody said anything for a minute. Trinvilla made a to-do about pouring coffee. I suppose she learned how to pour real fancylike from all those ladies' meetings she went to in church. She was getting notions, that's what her problem was. Thought she was too good for us anymore.

"What does Johnse want from Ro?" I asked the preacher.

"Just to see her. As I said, he's heard she's failing."

"He loves her still, Fanny," Trinvilla put in.

I scowled. "I suppose there's no sense in asking why you care, when you always hated Ro."

Her smile was like a knife. It was kindly but bespoke things between them that I was too young to understand. "We were all children back then, Fanny," she said. "We're all grown now."

"Johnse can be grown as last year's corn. There's no way he can come into Kentucky and see Ro without his being killed," I told her.

"He's been here many times," the reverend said.

"To this house?" I asked.

The reverend stirred sugar into his coffee. "Haven't you ever seen the man in the wool hat in the rowboat on the river? He's seen you. Said you waved to him many a time."

Now I felt like I was out in the windy night, looking in the window at them. The man in the woolen hat? Johnse Hatfield? "Why did he never give me his howdy if it was him?"

"He didn't want to put you in a compromising position."

"What's that?"

"He didn't," Trinvilla explained, "want to make you waver between telling Pa he was there and loyalty to him."

"I've got no loyalty to Johnse Hatfield," I said.

"Does that mean you won't deliver the note to Ro, then?" the reverend asked.

"I don't know what it means. I have to study on it."

He put his hand inside his coat pocket and something crackled. Paper. He drew out the note and set it on the table next to me. "Why don't you leave it to your sister if she wants to see him."

"Why don't *you* deliver the note to Ro?" I asked him.

"I have to leave for Pennsylvania in the morning. My sister is dying. It will be an extended stay."

"Where would this meeting take place? He'd come in his wool hat on the river and expect her to come sashaying down the bank in the cold and dark?"

"In this house," the reverend said. "It is a safe house. Neither side comes here."

"It'll be right cold soon," Will put in. "And the fall rains will come, making the roads muddy. There's no way we could justify a trip here for an ailing Ro if we wait much longer."

They were all in on it. Had it planned. It was why they'd invited me. Not because they cared about me. I took the note from the table and put it in my pocket. *Safe house?* I almost laughed in their fool faces. I'd come, and look what had happened. I'd been lured, trapped. Crazy, they all were, I decided. Plumb crazy.

Chapter Thirty-Five

FALL 1889

I SUPPOSE I could have done it. What reason not to? After I got shut of my anger at prissy old Trinvilla, who was turning out worse than Alifair had ever been, who still hated Ro and was just playing some part for her reverend father-in-law, I saw no reason not to do it.

I went home set on doing it. What did I care if Ro and Johnse met? What did I care about any of them anymore? Look what caring had done to me. I was mooded up all the time and worrying, and there was Trinvilla, happy and loved and out of it all, yet feeling good about herself. It meant no nevermind to her if Ro and Johnse met. Why should it matter to me?

Then I looked at Ma, all crippled up and scarce able to walk. I thought of Bud, Bill, Pharmer, Tolbert, Calvin, and even Alifair. All of them lying underground. All who should still be living. Even Alifair, mean as a hornet as she'd been. And I thought how I couldn't dishonor them like that by bringing together the two people who had started this whole mess. So I went home and put the note under my pillow, ate supper, saw to Ro, and went to bed, as muddled in the head as I'd ever been.

Next day Dr. Grey came to visit Ro. Ma had sent for him. He was in that room awhile with her, I can tell you. Then he talked awhile with Ma. I waited in the parlor to see him out. On the front stoop I drew a shawl around me in the late September chill and squinted up at him in the midday sun. "How's Ro faring, Doctor?"

"Well, I'll tell you, Fanny, 'cause you're old enough to know. How old are you now?"

"Sixteen."

"Your ma's not fit to hear it. Your pa's not around, and Ro seems not to care. I think if you all could get her interested in something, might be she'd take a turn for the better."

"Interested?"

"She's dying inside her, Fanny. Dying from the inside out. The worst kind of ailment. Nothing a doctor can do for her. She needs hope."

I nodded. Sounded like so much folderol to me. Like the kind of thing doctors said when they couldn't cure you.

"I know you all been through a heap of trouble, but your sister just needs something now to make her want to get well."

"What?" I asked.

"She's your sister, Fanny." He patted my arm. "Now I've got to go."

So that's when I decided to give her the note that lay at that moment in my apron pocket. That's when I decided to dishonor Tolbert, Pharmer, Bud, Bill, Calvin, and Alifair. They'd want me to do it, I pondered. Even Alifair. I was sure she would.

I waited all day, but Ma was always around. Then some snoopy old ladies from the church came, not Reverend Thompson's church but the Baptist one in town. Brought food and baked goods and we had to fuss over them and be nice. And then Ro slept and I didn't want to bother her. Then it came around to suppertime and I had to see to it that Ma ate and get her to bed. I went to my room and, while I waited for Ma to fall asleep, I fell asleep, too, and awoke like somebody put a hand on me to hear a noise downstairs. I jumped up, real scairtlike. Were we being attacked? I crept down the stairs and there in the kitchen was Ro in her nightdress, walking around with a lantern in her one hand and dragging something that looked like a dead body in the other.

"What are you doing up and about?" I asked her. "What have you got there?"

"Oh, Fanny." She set the lantern on the kitchen table. "I just had a hankering for some tea. I couldn't sleep. I thought I'd come down here for a while and work on my quilt."

So that's what she was dragging around. Might as well have been a dead body. I made her some tea. The candlelight threw our shadows against the wall, larger than life. I wondered if Johnse was out on the river in his boat, wearing that wool cap, watching the house. Wondered how many times he'd been out there and we hadn't known it. I set the tea down.

"You're so good to me, Fanny," she said.

I got to feeling all twisted inside when she said that, I can tell you. She was lifting the quilt from the floor and spreading it on her lap. "Hard to work without a frame, but I've gotten used to it. I just do a little piece at a time. Hard to work in candlelight, too. I wish Ma would allow kerosene."

I still had the note in my pocket. This was the time to give it to her, I minded. Now. Then she looked up at me, all hollow around the eyes and thin in the face, and smiled. "Want to ask you something, Fanny."

I nodded.

"Are you ready now to promise to take my quilt? I asked you once before. You said you'd study on it. Don't say no, please. It means so much to me. I know you don't like it. Don't approve. But I want it to go to somebody I love."

"You're not going to die," I said. It was all I could think of. My throat wasn't working right. I loved Ro. Much as I ever had, I suppose. And I hated her all at the same time. She'd always been the special one in the family, the one everybody gave in to. Because she was so purty. I'd looked up to her so. And now here she sat, empty and pitiful, the cause of all our troubles. Oh God, I wanted to give her that note. I did!

"You see here?" She was bent on showing me that fool quilt. "Look how purty it is. I *am* going to die, Fanny. I've got nothing to live for. Don't want to live anymore, anyways. A person can will themselves to die, you know."

I thought of Bill then and how sweet he could play the fiddle. How he'd frozen to death on that hill by the graves, willing himself to die. And I hated her again.

She had the quilt spread on the table. Her work was so neat, her stitches so small. "Isn't it a beauty?" she asked.

I looked. And I saw. There, in the light of the candle, among the coffins all around the edges that still had to be moved to the middle, was mine. And hers and Ma's and Pa's. Jim's and Sam's and Floyd's. Trinvilla's and her baby's. Tolbert's baby Cora.

I stared at them and felt the rage go through me. Then I looked up at her smiling at me like that, and I saw the bones in her face without the flesh, the eye sockets without the eyes, the teeth without the lips. Grinning at me. "Ain't it purty?"

I saw in the light of the single candle what I had known inside me all along.

Ro was kin, somehow, to evil. She courted it, beautiful as she was. There was something about her that flirted with it, like moths flirted with flames. That day of the election so long ago now, when she'd gone off with Johnse, she'd been flirting with it. Much as she'd been flirting with him. She sought destruction of herself. And she'd dragged so many of us with her.

In that moment I knew I would never give her the note from Johnse. And I recollected what Mr. Cuzlin once told me: "Sometimes we don't have to leave to get away. Sometimes we just have to choose." I chose.

I loved her. I still did. But I knew that the best thing in the world for all of us would be to get away from her before she did more destruction.

If I gave her the note and she went to Trinvilla's to meet Johnse, bad would come of it. Somebody would find out. And there would be more death. Maybe Trinvilla this time. Or her husband or baby.

"I'd love to have the quilt," I told her. "Now why don't you finish your tea and I'll take you up to bed."

Epilogue

I BURNED THE note the next day. I was supposed to send one to Trinvilla and Will and let them know when to fetch Ro, but the note I sent two days later said she was too sickly to travel.

They didn't come 'round. I didn't reckon they would. They'd never been to see us at the Pikeville house. Didn't want to dirty their hands by coming. Maybe they were right, I don't know. Maybe they saw things as they were long before I did. I don't fault them for it. In the trouble, we all had to find our own way out the best we could. Do what we had to do to survive.

Ro died a month later. Willed herself to. The night before, I was in the kitchen locking up when I saw a light out back. I looked out, thinking, *Oh, I hope it's not Johnse come anyway in his old wool hat.* And when I looked, he was there, just outside the window.

Yeller Thing.

I couldn't believe it was him, come all the way from our old homeplace! I hadn't seen him in two years! How'd he find us here? Did I have to ask?

I opened the door and went outside. I wasn't scairt. I felt about him like an old friend now. I knew he wouldn't harm me. "She's a-goin' to die tonight, isn't she?" I asked him.

He just lowered his head, his tongue all lolling out like he'd traveled a long way. But those eyes, how they glowed! And the smell of him! Then he did a strange thing. He lowered himself down like a lost dog and rested his head on his paws, all greenish yellow and ugly as can be. *Why, he is pure tuckered out,* I thought. And I knew then that it was the last time I would see him.

"I thank ye for the warning," I said. And then I went into the house and upstairs to check on Ro. She was sleeping real peaceful-like. She wasn't feverish. I looked out the back window from the hall. Yeller Thing was gone.

Next morning Ro never got out of bed at all. I went upstairs to find her dead. Pa buried her in Dils Cemetery, other side of Pikeville. He never said why he didn't take her back to Blackberry Fork and bury her with the others. We didn't ask.

I think I knew.

I think we all did, though none of us ever spoke the words. I think might be I was the last one to know about Ro and what she was about. But I thank God I came around to knowing.

All the newspapers carried news of her death. They played it up, all the things we'd rather forget. How

Roseanna McCoy was the one who caused the feud between the two families, how a war had been fought over her. Like Helen of Troy. Imagine! My sister!

Trinvilla and Will didn't come to the funeral. Reverend Thompson was still in Pennsylvania. Johnse Hatfield didn't come, either. None of the Hatfields came. I think my family would have killed them right over her gravesite if they did.

Might be if I'd given her the note she would have rallied. I think of it as saving more lives. Though at night when the house is quiet I mind that I probably killed her by not giving it.

I think how strange this fight was between our families. How the killings, the raids, the maiming, the burning, and loss of property and home was all so bad. But the things we didn't do when we should have were just as bad.

Ma didn't give Jim permission to send for Pa and form a posse. I didn't give Ro the note from Johnse. People who knew didn't tell the judge that Ellison Mounts wasn't to blame for killing Alifair. And the wrong man was hanged. Oh, I tried to tell Pa. We had a regular fuss about it. But he wouldn't hear it. "Somebody has to hang for killing Alifair," he said. I told him it wasn't right, that I'd go to the judge myself, and he laughed and said no judge would listen to a woman, look how they'd called Ma a liar in court, and she was there. So I knew he was right.

The things we don't do are just as bad as the things we do in this life. It can drive you pure daft, if you think about it.

I have thought about it. A lot. Which is maybe why I've told Mr. Cuzlin I want to take that exam and get into normal school. And try to become a teacher. Might be some good will come of it that wouldn't be if I just sat around here taking care of Ma every day and brooding. Ma will get taken care of. Let Adelaide come home and stay for a while. I've decided to do it.

Think on it. Something good coming out of something a McCoy did. That's a hoot, isn't it?

I've not seen Yeller Thing again and I don't expect to. I still have Ro's Coffin quilt. And someday soon I'll burn that, too.

AUTHOR'S NOTE

——

ALTHOUGH THERE HAVE been other famous feuds in America, the Hatfield-McCoy feud is the most famous and widely recognized. Like most recognizable events in our history, it has now been elevated to the realm of folklore. Having achieved this status, there are many versions and interpretations, the most popular being that it started in 1880 when Roseanna McCoy of Pike County, Kentucky, ran off with Johnse Hatfield of West Virginia.

However, by 1880 the bad blood was already evident between the Hatfields and the McCoys. Some say it started during the Civil War (what the clans in West Virginia and Kentucky then called The War Amongst Us) when Ranel McCoy's younger brother Harmon, who had come out for the Union, was home on leave and killed by West Virginia bushwhackers who were Hatfields as well as Confederates, men who had come home to find that their part of the state had pulled away from the rest of Virginia and become Union.

Was this when the seeds for the bad blood were planted? Nobody knows. But we do know that the Civil War conditioned men who fought in it to kill and to hate, and that in many instances they went right on hating and killing after it was over. This happened especially in the West, where it gave rise to many notorious guerrilla gangs or gunfighters. And in this far-flung region of the country, the West Virginia–Kentucky border, where nobody kept count of who was doing what, where the mountain people held to their own code of ethics. So in actuality we can say this feud was a continuation of the war.

At any rate, the bad feelings that rose from the killing of Harmon McCoy smoldered and surfaced again after the war in 1878 when Ranel McCoy lost his hogs, which he alleged were taken by Hatfields. A trial followed and Ranel McCoy lost. The enmity that ensued here was kept under control, apparently, until the elections of 1880, when Roseanna McCoy, Ranel's prettiest daughter, ran off with Johnse Hatfield, the handsome son of Anse Hatfield, nicknamed "Devil Anse."

Ranel McCoy considered this act a betrayal by his daughter and revenge against him by Devil Anse, and the feud was fed by it and went on with fighting and killings becoming a way of life for both families until 1889. Hatfields and McCoys took to shooting each other on sight. Arrests in home territories always resulted in acquittals, since every other deputy was a relative of the family on their home turf. Posses were constantly formed by both parties to cross and recross the Tug Fork of the Big Sandy River and invade "enemy" land. As the feud gained momentum, farming was neglected and land was sold off to get money to invest in hiring detectives, to pay hired guns, and to buy ammunition.

The worst of the bloodshed happened on New Year's Eve in 1887, when Hatfields attacked Ranel McCoy's house on Pond Creek on the Blackberry Fork in Kentucky. The open gunfire of the raid caused the deaths of Ranel's daughter Alifair and his son Calvin. During the battle Ranel's wife, Sarah, was beaten and nearly killed, and the house was burned to the ground.

Newspaper accounts called this New Year's Eve attack worse than any ever committed by Indians on the pioneers, the worst in Kentucky's history.

Yet somehow, after all the killings and hatred, the warfare between the two clans eventually ended. One possible reason was the advent of commercial coal mining in the area. Developers would not abide such behavior and pressured the law to end it. Some even offered a reward for the capture of old Devil Anse, who hid out in the hills until he died in 1921.

The feud, which had lasted so long in the steep and rugged ridges of the West Virginia–Kentucky border, was over.

Hatfields became respectable mine operators. McCoys went back to their lives, too, cultivating the land, raising ginseng, keeping bees, breeding cattle, hogs, and sheep, and displaying many of the traits and talents the people of these parts are famous for—the traits that mark the pioneer, the survivor, the breaker of the land, the raiser of the family, the churchgoer, the good neighbor. The most famous American family feud disappeared into the annals of American folklore, and today most people may recognize the Hatfield-McCoy names, but know nothing about them at all.

WHEN I TOOK on the project of this novel I immediately saw how vast and far-reaching the story was. So I knew I had to contain it. If one does factual reading about the feud, one will discover that many characters involved in it, but not central to the telling, are not in this book. I could not encompass everything in the Hatfield-McCoy story. For instance, where was Josephine, the oldest in the McCoy clan, born in 1848? She does not figure in the feud and was apparently married and gone from the area, so I did not involve her. The same went for Lilburn, a son born in 1856, so I have him off "seeking gold."

I made Fanny, the youngest, the protagonist, because she was just the right age to tell the story in 1889, and her recollections, which go back to a child of seven and, in one instance, earlier, are viewed and processed as a child would see things. Obviously, with her siblings being all ages, the story would vary and the interpretation be different if told from the eyes of any of them.

I have followed religiously the chronology of events—the stealing of Ranel McCoy's hogs, the trial that followed, the meeting of Johnse and Roseanna at the elections of 1880, the killing under the pawpaw trees, and everything else that is rooted in history. But, as with all my books, the when and where means little if you don't have the why of it. And the why of it is not supplied in history. We can only guess at the emotions that compel people to do what they do. But the why of it is what makes up historical fiction.

So, as with all my books, I have supplied the why. For instance, there is nothing in my research that tells me that Alifair and Fanny didn't get on, but there is Fanny, the youngest in the family. And there is Alifair, twenty-nine and still living at home when she is shot on New Year's Eve in 1887. Why is she still single and living at home when most young girls in these hills were wed at sixteen? Well, she must have had a distinctive character. Perhaps she was too strong willed. Or perhaps she was intent on pursuing some interest that meant more to her than marriage. So I made her a "healer." Yet, not having wed, she would be wanting to see to the household in the ways of a woman, and with her mother sickly, she would want to take over the McCoy kitchen. And part of that would be bossing around little Fanny, maybe even picking on her and taking out all her frustrations on her. So I have the tension between Fanny and Alifair.

The characters of all the others in the family pretty much follow where history leads me. Big brother Jim was a sheriff's deputy. I gave Floyd the occupation of running the still and making toys and the others duties of raising bees and hunting because in a family of this size everyone would have had their own chores based on their talents or specialties.

Therefore, as with every historical novel, the interaction of the characters is my own invention. The characters are mine, after history gives me what it knows about them. Yet I made up little. I did not have to. The story is enough in itself. Sarah McCoy, the mother, was overreligious and did hold back her husband from running raids against the Hatfields many times. She did beg Devil Anse Hatfield for the lives of her boys at the schoolhouse and promise not to send for her husband, based on his promise to her, which he did not keep.

Ambrose Cuzlin, Fanny's teacher, is just about the only character of my own invention, although he is a composite of teachers of the time and place. Yeller Thing is a mythical creature of my own invention also, although ghosts, boogers, witches, and haints were very much a part of the culture of this time and place. Tales of eerie encounters were told and retold around the old stove or fireside at night. In these heavily wooded mountains, where actual panther cats, snakes, and bears waited to harm humans and Bible reading was a regular daily activity, superstition seems to have reigned. Death affected the whole community because people needed the support of their neighbors in those days. They supported each other in bad times and celebrated together in good times. The enemy could be nature, the weather, bad crops, a black bear, a wild hog, fire, or a scream in the woods at night that could be a panther cat or a witch on a rampage.

People knew evil when they saw it. They planted by signs; some were healed by faith, others by natural remedies. If you feared something you made a cross in the dirt with your toe, spit in it, and made a good wish before you left the house. This is only one of many superstitions that got people through a time when there might be no doctor, there were no medicines, sometimes no schools, and little information filtering into their lives from the outside world.

According to my research there really was a Belle Beaver in the area at the time, a "fallen woman" who was driven out. Her role in the story is of my own making.

In history, the feud just quietly came to an end one day. I have Fanny in the possession of a note from Johnse to be given to her sister Roseanna when she is dying. Roseanna, in actuality, just seems to have withered away, as if she willed herself to die. As did brother Bill, after Bud was killed.

As for the Coffin quilt—it was a unique quilt made by women in these parts. Women made quilts to satisfy artistic as well as practical needs. A pioneer girl learned to use the spinning wheel, loom, and needle while young. It was part and parcel of her education, along with keeping house, cooking, caring for livestock, and planting a kitchen garden. Girls started making "kiverlids" or coverlets at a young age. In my book, Roseanna didn't have one when she met Johnse. She was too busy being popular and attending social events. So when she stayed at the Hatfields she took up the Coffin quilt, which has meaning on several levels. It is not only to serve as a warm bed comforter for her and Johnse, it is the symbol of her hoped-for marriage, and of the death and destruction that her relationship with Johnse comes to represent. Indeed, of all the mountain crafts practiced by these very inventive and talented people of Kentucky and West Virginia, the Coffin quilt, which to them served as a kind of record of family births and deaths, stood out for me as unique and representative of this feud, which in scope, individual foibles, passions, and strengths rivals anything in classical Greek tragedy.

BIBLIOGRAPHY

Donnelly, Clarence Shirley. *The Hatfield-McCoy Feud Reader, by Shirley Donnelly.* Parsons, W. Va.: McClain Printing Company, 1972.

Eastman, Mary, and Mary Bolté. *Dark and Bloodied Ground.* Riverside, Conn.: Chatham Press, 1973.

Federal Writers' Project of the Work Projects Administration for the State of Kentucky. *Kentucky, a Guide to the Bluegrass State.* New York, N.Y.: Harcourt Brace & Company, 1939.

Gillespie, Paul F., ed. *Foxfire 7: Ministers, Church Members, Revivals, Baptisms, Shaped-note and Gospel Singing, Faith Healing, Camp Meetings, Foot Washing, Snake Handling, and Other Traditions of Mountain Religious Heritage.* New York, N.Y.: Anchor Books/Doubleday, 1982.

McCoy, Truda Williams. *The McCoys: Their Story as Told to the Author by Eye Witnesses and Descendants.* Pikeville, Ky.: Preservation Council Press of the Preservation Council of Pike County, 1976.

Stuart, Jesse. *Men of the Mountains*, 1941. Reprint, with a foreword by H. Edward Richardson, Lexington, Ky.: The University Press of Kentucky, 1979.

Waller, Altina L. *Feud: Hatfields, McCoys, and Social Change in Appalachia, 1860–1900*. Chapel Hill, N.C.: The University of North Carolina Press, 1988.

Wigginton, Eliot, ed. *The Foxfire Book: Hog Dressing, Log Cabin Building, Mountain Crafts and Foods, Planting by the Signs, Snake Lore, Hunting Tales, Faith Healing, Moonshining and Other Affairs of Plain Living*. New York, N.Y.: Doubleday, 1972.

———. *Foxfire 2: Ghost Stories, Spring Wild Plant Foods, Spinning and Weaving, Midwifing, Burial Customs, Corn Shuckin's, Wagon Making and More Affairs of Plain Living*. New York, N.Y.: Anchor Books/Doubleday, 1973.

———. *Foxfire 3: Animal Care, Banjos and Dulcimers, Hide Tanning, Summer and Fall Wild Plant Foods, Butter Churns, Ginseng, and Still More Affairs of Plain Living*. New York, N.Y.: Anchor Books, 1975.

———. *Foxfire 4: Water Systems, Fiddle Making, Logging, Gardening, Sassafras Tea, Wood Carving, and Further Affairs of Plain Living*. New York, N.Y.: Anchor Books, 1977.

———. *Foxfire 6: Shoemaking, Gourd Banjos and Song Bows, One Hundred Toys and Games, Wooden Locks, a Water-powered Sawmill, and Other Affairs of Just Plain Living*. New York, N.Y.: Anchor Books/Doubleday, 1980.

Wiggingon, Eliot, and Margie Bennett, eds. *Foxfire 9: General Stores, the Jud Nelson Wagon, a Praying Rock, a Catawban Indian Potter, and Haint Tales, Quilting, Home Cures, and the Log Cabin Revisited*. New York, N.Y.: Anchor Books/Doubleday, 1986.